UNDER HIS SPELL

SELENA COLLINS

ENDLESS ROMANCE PUBLISHING

Published by Endless Romance Publishing

First Edition August 2025

ISBN 978-1-963671-05-6 (paperback)

ISBN 978-1-963671-04-9 (ebook)

SelenaCollins.com

*To all the Beauty and the Beast baddies who wanted the library
and **the** beast just as he was.*

CONTENTS

1

Emily Hartwell stood on the doorstep of Moore Manor with nothing but a bundle of nerves in her belly and a blanket of cold air wrapped around her. She looked up at the dark mansion towering above her and shivered despite the warmth of the season, a chill slipping under her skin with icy fingers.

It sat at the forefront of the sprawling estate, an homage to European architecture that seemed to breathe in and out, stirring the air around it so that the trees bent and whispered to each other in the shadows. Emily imagined it was once quite grand, though time had been a cruel mistress. Stone gone dark from age, bright green vines twisting into dead growth, and wooden framing that was cracked and split made it seem more haunted than impressive.

Emily fixed a professional smile on her face and rang the doorbell, the sound echoing through the air like a warning. She may be an under-funded scholar with a less than glamorous day job, but she didn't have to act like one.

Finally, the heavy doors creaked open to reveal an imposing figure standing on the other side. The man before her had the kind of presence that made the air feel thick and unyielding. His shoulders filled the doorway, and his stern expression invited little in the way of pleasantries, let alone idle chit-chat.

Devlin Moore stood at over six feet tall, his broad frame filled out by years of pent-up frustration and silence. Dark hair, once neatly combed, now fell in messy waves around his sharp face, a face that appeared as if it was carved from stone by one of the masters. His eyes—dark, like a storm on the horizon—scanned her all at once, calculating, assessing her.

Unnerving her.

"Ms. Hartwell?" His voice was deep, gravelly, like he hadn't used it in some time.

The roughness made her stomach twist, but she refused to be deterred. She had some pride, of course, but a girl also had to eat, and she desperately needed the paycheck this job would bring.

"That's me. Mr. Moore, I'm assuming?" She tried to steady her breath as she took in his appearance... all of it. Her smile only faltered for a moment, betraying the slightest flicker of uncertainty, but she hoped he wouldn't notice.

He nodded, stepping aside to let her in, his movements slow, deliberate, like each one took more effort than it should. She followed him through the large, darkened entryway, where the dim light only accentuated the mansion's opulence.

Heavy velvet curtains hung like dark waves along the walls, and the floor beneath her feet was marble—cold and unwelcoming. The home seemed well-suited to its owner.

"Follow me," Devlin said, his voice low as he turned. He walked with a confident, almost angry, stride. His jaw was square, and he wore a frown that only softened when he spoke, however brief his words may be.

As Emily moved down the hall, a haunting portrait of a woman in Victorian garb loomed on the left side, its eyes watching her every step. She fought against the shiver that slicked down her spine. She could feel the house seeping into her bones, but she didn't let it show. There was a weight to the place—the years, the history, the silence—and it unnerved her.

Walking through the endless winding halls, Emily wondered how she would ever remember her way around. The air grew heavier, thicker, like the house itself was trying as hard to smother her as it was to get her lost. Still, her anxiety didn't prevent her from noticing the intricate details on the wood paneling or the ornate sconces the decorated the walls. It wasn't simply the beauty that called to her. It was the overwhelming loneliness that clung to the space, like a forgotten echo dancing up and down these halls forever, never finding ears to listen or voices to answer.

At last, they stopped in front of a set of large double doors, and she could have sworn they were back at the front of the house. Devlin turned to face her, his gaze locking with hers. He raised a brow as if he knew exactly what she was thinking and was challenging her to say it.

"As I told the agency, the house desperately needs attention. There are parts that are simply unusable now and no one left to tend to it. You're here to do just that, to organize the house quickly and quietly," he said, his voice almost mechanical, as though he was dealing with a task long put off. "I want to preserve certain parts of it—the items that pertain to my family's heritage, our legacy—but I don't intend to be involved in that process." He paused, eyes narrowing. "That's your job."

Emily blinked. "What parts of the house am I to work on?"

"Not every room, but most of them, I would expect. You'll learn what needs attention easily enough. The agency assured me your background lent itself to a certain level of... discernment." His tone darkened at the last word, as if he was trying to convince himself more than her. "I'm sure you'll find that skill useful."

She swallowed hard, not sure what to say. There was a story hidden behind his words, something far deeper than just wanting to organize and preserve family heirlooms. She was sure of it.

"You'll start in the library," he said, throwing open the doors in a single motion.

Emily stepped into the room and gasped. There was no

other way she could react. The room was vast, with towering shelves packed with books of all kinds. Leather-bound volumes, faded hardcovers, ancient looking texts that seemed to whisper secrets of the past, modern paperbacks of all genres. They were all mixed together, strewn about tables and chairs among a treasure trove of papers, journals, and what looked like photo albums.

On one side of the room, there stood the only relatively clean table with stools arranged haphazardly around it. Opposite that, a row of velvet chairs flanked a foreboding fireplace, the stone cold and unused from flames long extinguished.

The air smelled of musty paper and old wood, a scent that made Emily feel transported back in time. This library was more than just a room; it was a shrine to Devlin's family, to his history, and to whatever burdens he carried.

"I'll get to work right away," Emily said, taking a step forward and surveying the room. Her fingers brushed over the spines of the books as she glanced back at Devlin.

He didn't respond. Instead, he stared at her, his jaw tight, as if he were waiting for something, waiting for her to do something, though she couldn't guess what. Perhaps he was waiting for her to say something else, ask the right question, even do something wrong.

Emily felt a brief spark of frustration. This wasn't a simple task; this was about more than books. She knew that. But she couldn't yet crack through the surface to understand the weight behind his cold exterior. Maybe she never would. Some stories weren't meant to be told.

She pushed the thought aside and focused on the bookshelves first. "Do you want this done in any particular way?"

Devlin took a long pause before responding, his gaze flickering over the room. "Preserve what matters—the family items, journals, letters, photographs, that sort of thing. Despite the chaos in this room, you will find each section labeled. Organize or discard anything else. I trust you'll be able to tell the difference." He spoke slowly, as if there were some hesitance. Emily caught the faintest trace of vulnerability, maybe, or regret, but it was gone too quickly to be sure.

"Don't allow your curiosity to interfere with the job you're being hired to do. You're here to restore order to these rooms, and that is all."

The look on his face told her he would not discuss it further.

"Understood," she said.

She got to work right away, doing her best impression of ignoring him as she moved about the room. She began by stacking books carefully and organizing them by genre. Any papers or photographs she came across were moved to another table to be sorted later.

As she worked, the weight of the silence between them grew. It was an unspoken tension, a heaviness she couldn't quite explain, and she wished he would just go already.

The more time went by, the more she caught herself glancing at him as he stood near the door. His posture was tense, as though he was afraid of being too close or too comfortable in the place he insisted on being.

Unable to ignore the curiosity that bubbled inside her, Emily broke the silence. "Why this room first?"

Devlin's gaze flickered, and she might have crossed a line. The seconds stretched on, and she worried her lip, keeping her hands busy as best she could. He looked like he was about to dismiss her. Instead, he walked across the room, each step measured. He stopped in front of one bookshelf and ran his fingers along the spines.

"This room was my father's sanctuary. I never liked coming here," he said, his voice quieter now, more distant. He paused then, as if suddenly becoming aware that the mask had slipped. He cleared his throat, and it was back in place, his voice hard once more when he spoke. "As it is now, there is simply no way to find anything. My father was not an organized man. That is why this room first. If you must know."

It may have been fleeting, but Emily had seen the cracks in his façade—just a glimpse—but it was enough to make her heart race. She felt a strange impulse to reach out, to ask more, but she knew better than to push. He wasn't ready for that. Not yet.

So, she bobbed her head in acknowledgment and continued sorting the books, feeling the weight of the room pressing down on her. She glanced over her shoulder and caught his eyes once more.

"Thank you," she whispered, the tone of her voice saying far more than the simple words she spoke. This was why she loved this work, why she agreed to them at all. Well, outside of the need to put food in her belly and a roof over her head.

It may not be the secrets of some ancient culture she was uncovering in some university funded archaeological dig, but it was often the long buried secrets of a family in desperate need of peace. The reward of piecing together a story from the remains of someone's life was still there.

The silence between them grew, and he said nothing, made no indication of wanting to, but his eyes softened, and Emily thought she saw his eyes flicker with emotion before he turned and left the room without another word.

Emily took a deep breath, unsure of what to make of him. He was a mystery—a man who carried the weight of his past like a shadow, a man who had hired her to handle the remnants of his family legacy. Yet he couldn't bear to be near it as much as he couldn't stay away.

This was only the beginning, and she wasn't sure if she was ready to turn the page.

2

The library was vast, stretching from one end of the mansion to the other, with towering shelves that seemed to go on forever. Books of all shapes and sizes lined the walls, from ancient leather-bound tomes to more modern volumes that looked as though they hadn't been touched in years. The scent of old paper and wood filled the air, and the heavy silence pressed down on Emily as she worked.

At first, it was daunting—the sheer volume of books, the endless rows of forgotten knowledge, the family photos and letters scattered about without rhyme or reason. After several days of sorting, it was almost meditative. The quiet was soothing, and the rhythm of organizing the shelves allowed her mind to wander, to imagine the lives lived in this house, the stories told through these books.

Her fingers traced the spines as she worked, pulling books off shelves and making note of their condition, and finding their proper place. There was an order to it, a quiet comfort in the predictability of her task. Yet, beneath the calm surface, there was always something more—something lurking in the corners of the room.

It lurked in the shadows and the spaces between the family albums, journals, and personal items tucked into odd corners of the library, in the pages of books that didn't belong.

Today, as she dusted off a shelf near the back of the room, she came across an old leather-bound album, its edges frayed with age. Curiosity tugged at her, and she gently opened the cover. The pages inside were yellowed with time, filled with photographs of people she could only assume were Devlin's ancestors. They were all stoic, their eyes piercing through the lens with a kind of silent judgment. Each portrait was more weight, each face adding to the legacy Devlin carried.

Emily turned the pages slowly, her fingers grazing the delicate paper. She came across one image that made her stop. Staring back at her was a young boy with dark eyes standing beside a woman who looked remarkably like him. Her smile was warm, soft, a stark contrast to the sternness of every other photo she'd come across.

Her heart skipped a beat when she realized the boy was a young Devlin, his face the picture of an innocence that no longer existed, before he hardened himself against the world. The photograph was old but clear. Devlin had been different once. It was in his eyes. There was a lightness in them.

The sound of a door opening startled her, and Emily quickly closed the album, hiding it back behind the shelf where she had found it. She turned just in time to see Devlin standing in the doorway, his dark gaze fixed on her.

"You've been in here a while," he said, his voice quiet but pointed, like a blade held too close.

Emily met his eyes, her breath catching in her throat. There was something in his gaze, something that flickered just beneath the surface. It was unnerving, as if he could see the very thoughts running through her mind.

"I was just... organizing," she said, her voice a little too loud in the silence. "I came across an album." She felt her cheeks flush, but she held his gaze, unwilling to look away.

Devlin's eyes didn't soften. "I asked you not to go through my personal things," he said, his tone clipped. There was an edge to his words, a warning that Emily couldn't ignore.

"I'm sorry." She wasn't sure what else to say.

Combing through treasured heirlooms mixed among years of junk at a family's estate was satisfying for someone like her. If she couldn't use her degree to dig into humanity's past, she may as well find some satisfaction using it to dig into a family's.

No one had ever complained before. In fact, they were often flattered and honored, sometimes even surprised when she came across a piece of new family lore. She wasn't exactly sure what to do with this reaction.

But she had agreed to it. Much to her chagrin.

"You're right. I didn't mean to overstep," Emily replied,

her voice steady despite the tension. She stepped back from the shelf, hoping to create some distance between them, but Devlin didn't move.

"You did, though I believe you regret it now."

"Yes."

He stood in the doorway, watching her carefully, his jaw tight. "You'll stick to the work I've assigned you," he said, his voice low. "Nothing more."

She nodded, biting back the impulse to ask why he hired a stranger at all if his privacy mattered so much, why these items seemed to hold such weight.

"Understood," she replied, though she didn't fully understand. She wanted to—she wanted to know everything about him, the pieces of him he kept hidden behind walls, the things he didn't want to face. But there was no room for questions, not right now.

Devlin turned away, but before he left, he paused and glanced back at her. "Be careful," he said, his voice almost a whisper. "Some things... some things are better left alone."

His words sent a shiver down her spine, and Emily watched him leave, the door clicking shut behind him with a finality that left her feeling more uncertain than before.

"Like you?" she asked to the empty room.

She didn't know what it was about this house that made her feel both drawn to it and repelled at the same time. The longer she stayed, the more it felt like she was uncovering pieces of a story she wasn't sure she was ready to hear.

Sighing, Emily returned to the shelf, but the image of young Devlin lingered in her mind. She couldn't help but wonder about him. What had happened to that boy? What had turned him into the man who stood in front of her now, with walls so high she couldn't see over them?

Her hands moved automatically as she sorted through the books, and she couldn't shake the feeling that she was on the edge of something. Though would she be prepared for it when she fell? There were too many layers to Devlin, too many secrets buried in this house, and Emily couldn't help but wonder if she had just uncovered the first of many.

When it was nearly time for her to go home, Emily rolled her shoulders back and pressed her fingers into the base of her neck, trying to work out the knot that had taken up permanent residence there. The ache stretched across her upper back like a set of wings carved from stone, and her spine popped when she twisted to the left and right. The library was dimmer now, bathed in soft amber light from the sconces along the walls, and the dust motes hung lazily in the golden glow like suspended stars.

She was gathering her things when a soft knock on the doorframe made her turn.

A woman with sleek dark hair and a fitted blazer leaned in, one manicured brow arched. "Emily Hartwell?"

Emily nodded and offered a tired but polite smile. "That's me."

The woman stepped inside and extended a hand.

"Kara Voss. Mr. Moore's assistant. Mind sparing a few minutes before you head out?"

"Of course."

Kara gestured toward the hallway. "There's a bit of paperwork the agency forgot to send over. It'll only take a moment. I can show you to the study."

Emily followed her out of the library, grateful for a change of scenery and the chance to stretch her legs. Kara walked with confidence and precision, the kind of woman who likely never forgot a deadline or spilled coffee on her blouse. Her heels clicked softly against the marble as they turned down a hallway Emily hadn't yet explored, this one more refined and less foreboding than the wing she'd been working in all day.

The study at the front of the house was masculine and warm. Deep brown leather chairs sat before low bookshelves lined with ledgers and set the tone of the room. A decanter sat perched on a cart near the window, and it smelled faintly of tobacco and aged paper.

"Have a seat," Kara said, already walking around to the desk. She slid a manila folder across the surface. "Just a few forms and tax documents. Nothing dramatic."

Emily sat down and flipped through the paperwork, scanning each page with practiced efficiency. "You handle all this?"

"Pretty much anything Mr. Moore doesn't want to be bothered with," Kara said, and there was a glint in her eye that walked the line between pride and amusement.

"Scheduling, hiring, legal matters, accounting, damage control—if it ends in 'ing,' I've probably done it."

Emily smiled. "Sounds like he keeps you busy."

Kara inclined her head. "He does. We've been together a long time." Kara leaned back in her chair, watching her closely. "You're not what I expected."

Emily blinked, her pen pausing mid-signature. "Is that a good thing?"

Kara tilted her head. "You tell me. Most of the women who've crossed this threshold didn't arrive in practical shoes with a tote bag Post-it tabs."

Emily's back stiffened with the sudden implication. "I wasn't aware that was part of the job description."

"It's not." Kara smiled, but it didn't quite reach her eyes. "Just an observation."

Emily went back to the paperwork, her pen moving faster now. Her cheeks felt hot.

"He's been... polite. Professional," she said, choosing her words carefully.

Kara made a soft hum in the back of her throat. "Has he?"

Emily looked up. "Are you getting at something, Ms. Voss?"

Kara's smile widened, but it was sharp now, like the glint off the edge of a blade. "I've just seen the way he looks at you."

"There's nothing going on," Emily said flatly.

"Of course there isn't," Kara agreed smoothly. "Yet."

Emily set the pen down and folded her hands over the

papers. "Look, I don't know what you're insinuating, but I'm here to do a job. That's all."

"I'm sure you are." Kara rose and walked to the bar cart, pouring herself a small glass of something amber and sharp. She didn't offer Emily any. "Devlin Moore has a way of drawing people in. Especially pretty girls with curious eyes. He likes things he can't have. Or rather, he likes to take them anyway."

Emily's spine straightened. "That's not my problem."

"Isn't it?" Kara took a slow sip. "Men like him... they come with teeth. And you seem like the type who thinks she can tame a wolf if she just talks gently enough."

"You don't know what type of woman I am."

"True."

Emily's lips pressed into a thin line. "And what type are you?"

Kara's gaze sparkled, and she raised a brow. "The type who knows better."

Both sat and considered each other, and silence stretched between them.

Kara set her glass down and crossed back to the desk. Her voice was still low, but a hint of compassion softened it. She sighed. "He's not cruel. Not exactly. But Devlin doesn't do attachment. Not in any way that lasts. Women drift in and out of this house like wind through an open door. Some of them think they're different. They're not."

Emily's fingers curled slightly against the desk. "And you think I'm one of them?"

"I think you seem like a sweet girl with a good head on

her shoulders. Focus on getting in, doing your job, and going back to your life." Kara gathered the papers into a neat stack and slid them back into the folder. "It's an old house, almost like a living thing all on its own. It has a way of making people forget the rest of the world exists."

Kara's words settled like ash.

Emily stood, squaring her shoulders. She couldn't decide whether she was more angry at being called a girl or at being treated like an infant. "Thanks for the warning."

Kara didn't answer. She simply smiled, closed the folder, and returned it to the desk drawer.

As Emily stepped into the hall and walked toward the front of the manor, her heart was pounding harder than it should have been. Kara's words echoed in her mind, heavy and unsettling.

She wasn't here to fall for her employer. She wasn't here to get tangled up in the life of a man who walked like he carried secrets in his bones.

But still...

Part of her wanted to know exactly what it was he kept buried.

3

Devlin Moore sat in his expansive study, the papers in front of him blurring into one indistinct mass. It didn't matter. He hadn't paid attention to them in the past hour. His mind was on a certain woman.

He drummed his fingers against the wood of his desk, the rhythm of it matching the pulsing beat of his thoughts. The house was silent, oppressive in its stillness, and Emily's presence lingered in the air like a perfume he couldn't shake. She was a light bobbing through the dark hallways of his life. He thought he'd been ready to turn them on and see what hid in the shadows. Sophia had been dead for years now, their parents gone long before that.

He was wrong.

She was in the library again today. He heard her soft footsteps and the sound of her moving around even though she was impossibly far away. It was a feeling, a knowing. Little by little, she sorted through his past, and he didn't like it.

Why had he hired her anyway? He rarely enjoyed people simply existing in his personal space, let alone poking around his things. And with Emily, it felt different. It was more. She wasn't a body in his home; she wasn't just touching his possessions. She was touching pieces of him, and that scared the hell out of him.

Not that he would admit that to himself, at least not in so many words. He leaned back in his chair and scrubbed his hands over his face. There was no reason to feel this unsettled. She was the hired help, nothing more.

Despite that reminder, the thought of her in that library, digging through his life, sent a wave of unease through him. Disgusted with himself and frustrated by his fixation on her, he clenched his jaw and shoved the feelings to the back of his mind.

Sorting through the belongings of his long-dead relatives and being reminded of moments, however sweet or unsavoury, was not on his list of desired experiences at present. It needed to be done, and it would be. One way or another. If Emily was willing to take it on, he would leave her alone to do it.

He turned his attention back to the laptop on the desk to his left, sliding a finger over the touchpad to wake it. The screen lit up, ready to resume their work, but his body stayed frozen. The screen dimmed, and then it darkened completely once again.

He stared at the black screen, but it was her face he saw —the way she looked at him, the way she didn't flinch when he snapped at her. She was a puzzle he wanted to solve but couldn't. His gaze was intense. He was intense, but she didn't run from it. That intrigued him more than he cared to admit.

The door to the study creaked open, but Devlin didn't need to look up to know it was her. Emily's presence was an undercurrent in the room, soft but undeniable.

Inevitable.

"Mr. Moore," she said. Her voice was steady, but there was an edge to it that caught his attention.

He glanced up from the desk, his dark eyes narrowing as he studied her. She hovered in the doorway, her posture stiff and aloof, but her breath hitched when she met his gaze, and he mused at the direction of her thoughts. She made no other sign he had any effect on her, but then she didn't have to. He could see it. More than anxiety, there was curiosity. He was sure of it.

She wanted him to speak first. She wanted him to react. He could feel the challenge in the air, the friction that had been building between them since the moment she stepped into his home.

He said nothing at first, letting the silence fill the space between them. Letting her feel tension the way he felt it.

"I wanted to let you know that I'm working on the parlor right now. I haven't quite finished in the library, but I'm taking a break," she said, stepping further into the room. She shrugged. "It's a big task."

Devlin's gaze flicked over her, taking in the way she held herself. It was confident, poised. She was careful, but he could sense the raw energy in her, the way she kept pushing against the walls he'd built around himself. He wondered if she knew she was even doing it.

"Good," he said, his voice controlled. "Keep moving. There's more to be done."

Emily didn't move, though. She stood watching him with wide eyes, as if she were waiting for him to give her an opening. Maybe she thought she could handle him, see past the walls, past the emotions kept tightly coiled within him.

He was sure she'd seen the childhood photos by now, possibly read some of the diary entries from his mother or sister. Both had kept journals throughout their lives. She probably believed she understood him on some level.

"You're not afraid of me, are you, Ms. Hartwell?" The question slipped out before he could stop it, a challenge wrapped in the most casual of tones. But beneath it there was a sharp edge that made the hairs on the back of her neck stand up.

Her lips parted, and for a moment, he thought she might deny it. Instead, she held his gaze with an unflinching strength that surprised him. A small, almost defiant smile tugged at the corner of her mouth, as if she found the question amusing.

"No," she said. "I'm not afraid of you."

Devlin felt a flicker of desire. It burned low in his stomach. It was a feeling he didn't want to acknowledge, but he couldn't deny it. Her words, simple as they were, stirred him in a way that felt so similar and yet so foreign.

"Why not?" he asked, his voice taking on a rougher edge as he leaned forward in his chair. His gaze dropped to her lips, then slowly back to her eyes. He wanted her to be afraid of him. She may spend her days combing through what she thought his life had been like, who she thought his family was, but she didn't know the half of what had shaped him. She had no idea the kind of man he'd become.

Emily didn't step back, merely sucked in a quiet breath and stood her ground. "I see stoicism and distance, but not danger. Which, I'll admit, makes me curious," she said, her voice almost a whisper. "Curious about what makes you dangerous."

"What makes you think I'm dangerous?"

"I've been told things."

"Go on."

"I'm told you like the challenge of seeing what you can't have." Emily licked her lips. "And taking it anyway."

Devlin's jaw tightened at her words, and molten desire rolled through his body. He could feel the pulse of it in his veins, the heat simmering beneath the surface. She was pushing him, interested rather than reviled by whatever she thought she knew of his... habits.

Like a moth to his flame.

He pushed up from his chair, its legs scraping against the floor with a sharp screech. Emily didn't move, didn't blink. She just watched him, lips barely open, waiting for what he would do next.

"Do you think I take what I want, Emily?" Devlin asked, his voice a dark murmur as he moved closer and closer to her with every breath.

She didn't speak, just looked up at him with eyes wide, pupils dilated, and tongue darting across parted lips. The way she reacted to him only increased his desire, and he felt certain parts of his anatomy grow hard in response, straining against the seams of his pants.

"I don't know," she said, her voice soft but sure. "Yes, no... I don't—maybe..." She trailed off, her gaze flicking to his mouth and fixing there.

Devlin was upon her then, his hand catching the back of her neck and pulling her closer. His body was a wall of heat, and she could feel it, feel the raw power in him as he loomed over her.

In that moment, time stopped, and all that remained was the weight of desire between them. It was palpable, electric. His grip on her was firm, almost possessive, his fingers digging into her soft skin. He could feel the pulse of her heartbeat beneath his fingertips, the warmth of her skin where it met his. He leaned in, close enough that she could feel his breath on her lips, the weight of his gaze pulling her in.

"You have no idea," he whispered. He exhaled shakily, pressing the line of his body against hers so that there was no doubt about just how much he wanted to take her, to take what he shouldn't.

Emily's breath caught in her throat, a knot of desire hot in her belly. The sexual attraction was undeniable, a force that neither of them could ignore. She didn't want to back away, didn't want to shy away from it, even as a voice in the back of her mind told her she should.

Instead, she let herself linger, let the moment hang between them, dangerous and thrilling. She reveled in it, in the waves of electricity it sent pulsing through her system. She didn't back down from his desire, meeting it with her own and letting herself relax into the weight of him.

Devlin's eyes darkened, and for a moment it seemed he would take what he wanted right then and there. Then he released his grip on her neck and stepped back, the distance between them suddenly too wide, a slice of cold air wedged between them.

"Get back to work, Ms. Hartwell," he said. His voice was gruff, as though he were trying to regain control of himself.

Emily didn't move immediately, still caught in the aftermath of the moment. Her heart was pounding in her chest, her skin tingling where he had touched her. She should've said something, should've broken the silence, but all she could do was nod, her throat tight.

"Of course," she managed, her voice barely above a whisper.

Devlin walked back to his desk and stood with his back to her, his shoulders stiff with the effort of holding himself together. He pressed the flats of his palms down into his desk, the cool wood useless against the raging heat that filled him. He didn't look back when she quietly left the room, the door shutting behind her with a tiny clicking sound.

Suddenly, the house felt too still. It was stagnant and silent even as inside him, a storm raged.

4

The dim light of the cafe wrapped around Emily like a soft blanket, the coolness of the space a comforting contrast to the warm air outside. She was meeting Zoe—her closest friend—after a long day at work, and she was glad to escape the oppressive quiet of the manor, if only for a few hours.

Zoe sat across from her, her face bright with curiosity. They'd been friends for years, since Emily had moved to the city. Zoe had been there through the highs and lows. She'd been her sounding board, her escape, the one person who could always make her laugh, as cliché as that sounded. Emily was grateful for the normalcy Zoe provided, even if it was becoming harder to keep her world separate from the strange pull of Moore Manor.

"You're late," Zoe teased, stirring her coffee absently. "I thought you might have fallen into a pit of dusty books by now."

Emily laughed, the sound light and easy. "Maybe I did. It feels like it some days."

Zoe raised an eyebrow. "So, tell me about this mysterious mansion of yours. You've been there, what? A few weeks now?"

Emily settled into her chair, her eyes wandering around the cafe before returning to Zoe's expectant gaze. "It's... interesting. The work is tedious, but you know I enjoy that part of it. It's kind of meditative in a way. The library's massive, so there's always something to be done, though I do wish I could pore through some of the things I find. There's so much family history there, but it's just out of reach."

"What's the deal with the owner? Your Mr. Mysterious?"

Emily hesitated, her fingers wrapping around the warm cup of coffee. She traced the rim with her thumb while she considered how much to say. She hadn't told Zoe the full story yet. There wasn't any real reason, but there was a part of her that didn't want to share too much about Devlin. Or about the house, for that matter. The more fantastical side of her worried that talking about it too much would make it all feel too real.

"He's mysterious all right." Emily was quiet, and she paused to gather her thoughts. "He's distant, but not in the way you think. It's like he's trapped in this place, this legacy he can't escape. It's all so... heavy. You feel it the minute you step inside the house. Judging from the state of the house, he's been dealing with his family's past, their deaths, for a while. I don't even really know how long they've been gone."

Zoe rolled her eyes. "So, he's a brooding, tortured man? How original."

Emily snorted. "I'm not saying he's some misunderstood hero or anything. It's just there's this darkness to him. He's got this wall around him, but I can tell there's more to him than just... stiffness and control. He has this intensity about him, a heat."

Zoe sipped her coffee, her eyes narrowing in thought. "So, you're telling me there's more to the guy than his billionaire bad boy persona, and it's that he's traumatized, hot, and intense? And why aren't you in his bed already?"

Emily chuckled. "I almost was, I think, but he pulled away. I'm not sure why, but it's better if I try not to get caught up in it. He's my boss. Not to mention he's complicated, and I'm there to do a job. That's it. The last thing I need is to get involved with someone like him."

Zoe raised a brow. "Someone like him? Like the bad boy type or the rich bad boy type? Because jeez, woman. You know how many of us would swap places with you right about now?"

A flush bloomed across Emily's cheeks, and she tried to cover it with a quick sip of her coffee. "I know, I know. But it's a bad idea. Don't get me wrong, he's gorgeous, and yes, he's also stupidly wealthy. But his intensity is honestly a little scary. Hot, but scary. I think I'm just... intrigued. There's a tension between us, like a magnet that's always pulling me in. I'm not sure I want to get involved, and beyond the attraction, I don't think he wants me to either."

Zoe leaned forward, her eyes gleaming with mischief. "Attraction, huh? You sure it's not a little more than that? Because, girl, I know a thing or two about chemistry. And what you're talking about sounds like it's more than that."

Emily hesitated. She'd felt the pull, the dangerous attraction, but she was careful not to act on it. Devlin was exactly the type of man she had learned to avoid. He was arrogant, guarded, and impossible to read, so wrapped up in his own world that even when she caught glimpses of vulnerability, he was afraid to acknowledge it. She didn't know what would happen if she let herself get too close to him. The idea of getting tangled up in his darkness was as thrilling as it was terrifying.

"I don't know." Emily's voice was quieter now. "Maybe, but I get this feeling I make him uncomfortable. Most days he acts like he doesn't want me there at all, and then he looks at me like that..." She trailed off as her mind turned to the moment when his body was up against hers, his lips so close she could feel the heat of them on hers.

Zoe made a small sound of interest in the back of her throat, her brows furrowed.

"I just can't help feeling like there's more going on, like I'm there for more than just the job."

Zoe's gaze softened, the playful spark in her eyes fading to something more serious. "For what, exactly?"

"I'm not sure yet," Emily said, her brow furrowing as she thought back on the subtle—and not so subtle—hints

Devlin had dropped over the last few weeks. She couldn't quite put her finger on what was under the surface, but she felt it. "It's like I'm meant to help him with more than just cleaning up his family's mess. It's like he's testing me, watching me to see how far I'll go. But every time I get a little too close, he shuts me down."

Zoe leaned back, considering. "Maybe you're right. Maybe it's more than just organizing books. But then again, maybe you're using that big storytelling brain of yours to string together clues that don't actually go together. This isn't some library of a lost civilization you're going through. This is someone's actual life. All of it. It's probably not going to fit together into a nice, neat story. People aren't really like that."

Emily's head bobbed up and down slowly, her fingers relaxing around the coffee cup. "You're probably right. Why is it so much easier to imagine the lives of the dead than the ones living right in front of us?"

Zoe laughed. "Oh, that's easy, love. Because people are messy as hell!"

Emily smiled into her cup, taking a sip and letting the warm liquid flow over her tongue and relishing just how good it felt to get this all off her chest. Ms. Voss, Kara, was right. That house did something to you when you were inside. You didn't just walk inside. You stepped back in time, and shadows of mystery and romance and drama enveloped you.

"I think he's trying to keep me at arm's length," Emily said finally.

"Why do you say that?"

"Because there's this weird tension, like he's trying to keep me intrigued without letting me get too close. He wants me, I think. But he doesn't do anything about it."

"Do you want him to?"

"I'm afraid of what will happen if I do."

"Well, that settles it then. I'm driving you to work at least once. That way, when you don't come home one night, I'll know which basement to tell the cops to go look in."

"I'll be fine."

Zoe studied her for a long moment, her expression turning serious. "You've got to be careful, Em. Guys like that—guys who live in their own world, full of secrets—they're dangerous. You don't know what you're getting into."

"I know, I know," Emily said, looking down at her coffee. "I just have to see it through. Figure out the story, and see what happens. You know how I am."

Zoe gave a small, knowing smile. "You're in deeper than you think, girl."

Emily didn't answer. She just stared into her coffee. The steam had ceased to waft from it, and on its surface was an opaque swirl of white cream and froth spinning lazily around the cup. It mirrored the dance she seemed to find herself in with Devlin. A dance that, no matter how much she wanted to refute it, had the two of them lazily circling each other. She wondered what would happen when they finally collided.

5

Devlin Moore hated the sound of his own thoughts.

They were incessant whispers, like a chorus of voices begging for attention, and he could never drown them out. The house was quiet today. Not that it wasn't always quiet, but it felt emptier than usual. He wasn't sure why that unnerved him so much. Maybe it was because Emily's presence had become too familiar, like an echo that was louder when you removed everyone else from the room.

He hadn't wanted her here. He had wanted someone. That was true. But not someone like her. Not her.

She was supposed to be just another part of his family's legacy, another cog in the machine, but the longer she stayed, the harder it became to keep her at arm's length. That was dangerous, both for her and for him.

His fingers tightened around the glass of whiskey in his

hand. The amber liquid swirled inside as he stared out the window. It had been a long time since he'd let in anyone close enough to matter, let alone someone like Emily Hartwell.

She wasn't like the others. The women he normally entertained would typically of two varieties: high society socialites looking to play with fire before settling down to marriage and babies with the son of daddy's business partner... and those of the paid variety.

The former saw him as a plaything, the candle flame they ran their fingers through. If they were careful, they could play with fire without getting burned. They saw the house, the legacy, and they saw only the walls he'd built around himself, the carefully crafted mask he created just for their world. They didn't see the darkness beneath.

The latter knew more about the world he lived in far more often, one that knew what he was capable of and rewarded it. They were afraid of him.

But Emily was different. She lived in neither of those worlds. Yet she looked at him like she could see through it all, as if she weren't afraid of what she'd find.

He didn't know what intrigued him more—the fact that she had no fear, or that he found her innocence thrilling. The idea of taking it was like a drug, alluring and intoxicating.

The door creaked open behind him, and Devlin didn't need to turn to know it was her. He could feel her presence in the room, the air shifting with her quiet footsteps. He didn't move, didn't acknowledge her right away. Instead, he took another sip of his drink, letting the burn settle in his throat.

"Mr. Moore," Emily said, her voice soft but firm, like it always was when she needed something. It had become a kind of ritual, her voice cutting through the silence of the house, a reminder that she was there—he couldn't even try to pretend she wasn't.

Devlin turned slowly, leaning against the windowsill, his gaze meeting hers. She was standing in the doorway, her expression carefully neutral, though he could see the faintest trace of restlessness in her eyes that suggested she was no longer just here to work.

"What is it, Ms. Hartwell?" His voice was low and toneless, almost bored. He didn't want to be here, didn't want this conversation. What he wanted was to shove her up against the wall and shove himself inside her, but he couldn't let his tone betray that thought.

"I'm nearly finished for the day," she said, her hands clasped in front of her. She hesitated.

"And?" he asked.

"My roommate is coming to pick me up today, but she's, um, running a little late. I wanted to let you know in case you see her car drive up."

Devlin nodded, his gaze flicking over her, taking in the way she stood. She was always so composed, but there was an undercurrent to her, a hunger beneath that calm exterior. It didn't belong. She was meant to be rigidly organized, a high-strung Type A person, yet here she was.

Curious as a cat and fighting every instinct of self-preservation not to convey timidity.

She didn't fit in this house, not in the way he wanted her to. She wasn't supposed to see him like this, a man drowning in his own past, his own regrets.

But she had already seen him. She had already caught glimpses of the things he wanted to hide. No matter how much he wanted to deny it, she saw him every time she walked into his home, every time she touched a piece of his history.

"Did you prepare your friend for what the house will be like?"

"What do you mean?"

"You've been here for a while," Devlin said, his voice dropping lower as he took another sip of whiskey. "You've seen the way things are. How does it feel?"

Emily didn't hesitate. She stepped into the room, closing the door behind her softly. "It's... suffocating," she said, her eyes never leaving his. "But I didn't come here to pass judgment. I came here to help."

Devlin raised an eyebrow. "Help?" he repeated. "Help with what?"

She hesitated as if weighing her words carefully. "Help you move forward. Help you make peace with all of this." She gestured vaguely around the room, her eyes scanning the space to show she was speaking about more than just the study—it was the house, the history, the weight of everything he carried.

Devlin set the glass down on the edge of the desk.

"Peace? There is no peace here. There's just—" He stopped himself, a muscle in his jaw twitching. He refused to discuss it further.

But she didn't let it go. "I'm not here to fix that, but I can do more than simply cataloging and organizing. I can tell the story," Emily said, her voice steady. "Sometimes the story can bring the peace."

Devlin's eyes darkened, and for a moment, he looked at her like she was something he wanted to devour. His hand gripped the edge of the desk, his knuckles turning white as the impulse to do something, anything, surged through him.

She had no idea what she was asking.

"Do you even know what you're asking for?" he growled, the words slipping out before he could stop them. "The stories these walls could tell would horrify you. For me, it was just a regular day. You know nothing about what would bring me peace, Emily."

Emily flinched, but she didn't step back. "I don't need to know everything," she said, her voice quieter now, but her gaze unwavering. "I only need to know you're willing to face it. To let go of it."

"I'm not. Lock it away and leave me be."

Devlin stared at her for a long moment, the words hanging heavy between them. The space between them was charged with something neither of them could control. The attraction was undeniable, like a current that ran beneath every word, every glance. It made his skin prickle, made his body tense with a hunger he couldn't satiate.

It was dangerous, what they were doing. Dangerous for her. Dangerous for him.

But the way she looked at him, like she saw him—not just the mask he wore, but the man beneath it—made something inside him snap. He stepped toward her in one smooth movement, closing the distance between them, the heat of his body crashing into hers like a wave.

Emily didn't move, didn't run. She stood her ground, her breath shallow as she looked up at him, the desire clear in her eyes.

He could feel it, the pull. The undeniable need to claim, to possess, to destroy everything in his path. His hand came up, cupping her jaw gently, the roughness of his thumb brushing over her skin. The touch was possessive, but not violent—not yet.

"What if I told you I'm not the man you think I am?" he whispered, his breath hot against her lips. "What if I told you I'd destroy you if you stayed here too long?"

She didn't flinch. Instead, she leaned into his touch, her voice barely a whisper. "Then I'll stay longer."

Devlin's control nearly snapped. He jerked his hand from her jaw to her neck, his fingers digging into the tender skin. Her pulse raged against his hand, and she whimpered, her lips a breath away from his.

He wasn't sure if it was out of fear or desire. He hoped it was both.

With a groan, he pulled away, stepping back with a force that left them both sagging and breathless. His chest heaved as he looked at her, the weight of what they'd almost shared hanging between them like a threat. He didn't want this. Didn't want her here. And yet, it was all he wanted. She was embedded in his mind, in his veins, like a thorn.

"Go," he commanded, his voice hard, his body trembling with the effort of holding back.

Emily didn't move for a moment, torn between the desire to challenge his restraint and self-preservation. With one last look—soft but filled with something fierce— she turned on her heel and left the room, nose tipped ever so slightly in the air.

Devlin watched her through the open door, his ears straining until he heard the distant thud of the front door closing. His heart hammered in his chest, and he felt his body being pulled to the window. He could see the paved circular driveway and the landscaping that flanked one side of the entrance.

Just then a car pulled up, a modest sedan not unlike the one Emily herself drove. A woman got out, her dark hair styled in a messy bob and swinging with every step. This was the roommate Zoe, he presumed. Emily walked out to meet her.

He could tell by the stiffness of her body and the seething tension that seemed to emanate from her that she was far angrier than he'd realized. Her gestures were sharp, agitated even, and then Zoe's gaze jerked upward.

She couldn't know which window was his, or that he stood at it obsessively watching Emily's every movement.

And obsessive was exactly what it was. He was losing control, and he hated it. Hated most of all that he doubted he could rid his system of it with a wild tumble and sending her on her way. He couldn't slow down the train of possessiveness screaming toward him.

But now more than ever, he wasn't sure he wanted to.

6

The next morning, Emily arrived to the familiar scent of dust and old paper, the hum of the house surrounding her like a quiet echo of a life long past. Moore Manor was the kind of place that felt suspended in time—trapped between the past and the present, between memories and reality. Every room she stepped into seemed to hold its breath. The house watched her, waiting for her to uncover its secrets.

She stifled a yawn and rubbed the last remnants of sleep from her eyes. Against her better judgment, she'd stayed late the night before, the temptation to sift through old family albums in the library too great. Inside were pieces of Devlin's past she wasn't supposed to touch, and honestly, she'd tried to respect his wishes to the best of her ability. It wasn't her fault that the loose photos strewn about the room needed to be properly stored inside the appropriate albums.

She felt a tiny pang of guilt at just how long her eyes had lingered on the photographs, but they pulled at her in ways she couldn't explain. She hadn't told him about what she'd found, of course. Nor would she. Nothing good would come of it, as he'd likely dismiss her on the spot, leaving her without a paycheck and, even more importantly, without an ending to the story. Somehow the young boy in the picture, the boy who looked so much like him it was impossible to be anyone else, was once so full of innocence and hope.

She couldn't help wondering what had happened to him. What had turned Devlin from that little boy in the photo into the man who locked himself away in a dark mansion, surrounded by the ghosts of his family's legacy? And what even was that legacy, anyway?

Emily realized she knew alarmingly little about Devlin or his family. Clearly they were ridiculously wealthy, but he'd rarely left the mansion in the weeks she'd been employed, so it wasn't as if he was regularly brushing elbows with the local elite. Though perhaps he took part in those activities late in the evening after she'd already gone home. It was certainly possible. Still, solving that mystery left so many questions unanswered.

What happened to his family? How had they amassed their wealth? What in the hell did he do in his study all day?

Shaking herself from her thoughts, Emily determined to focus. She couldn't let herself get distracted by thoughts of Devlin or his past. She had work to do. The closer she got to finishing, the closer she would get to telling the whole story.

With the tables finally clear, Emily set herself to reordering the massive bookshelves. She pulled out stack after stack of books, dusted the shelves, sorted each stack, and then replaced them on the shelf. She worked methodically, not noticing how sore her arms were getting until her stomach grumbled loudly enough to startle her.

She stopped and took stock of her progress, amazed she'd gotten so much done. Though it was no wonder, she thought as she stretched her arms and worked the stiffness out of her lower back. Her stomach knotted and grumbled again.

"I suppose I should probably eat," she said to the empty room.

She brushed at the dust on her shirt and pants as she walked out of the library and made her way down the long hallway toward the kitchen. The walls seemed to press in on her from both sides. She told herself it wasn't real, this oppressive feeling, but she found her feet moving faster. The only sounds around her were that of her rasping breaths and the soft pit-pat of her shoes padding along the carpet runner.

She didn't expect to see anyone else, so when she passed by the parlor and caught sight of Devlin in her periphery, she jerked to a halt. His back was to her, but his mere presence was a surprise, and she pressed a hand into her chest as if that could calm her racing heart or quiet her too-fast breathing. Devlin was always elusive, always retreating into his study or his office when he didn't want to be found. She couldn't say she ever wanted to find him, but she wasn't upset that it happened. The sight of him sent a ripple through her body, an electric current that set her belly aflutter.

Emily watched him like a deer might watch the mountain lion, not spooked enough to run but certain that seeing him meant danger. He stood without moving, his posture and every joint held rigid. The room hummed with energy, a thick noise that filled her ears like cotton balls.

It unsettled her.

It excited her.

They were on the precipice of something. She wasn't certain if this was the moment that would change everything or not, but she couldn't imagine the simmering tension could escalate any more. It was there anytime they were close, a magnetic pull that was as exquisite as it was nearly unbearable.

She inched into the room, careful to keep her steps light. He didn't seem to hear her approach, but she didn't mind. She lingered close to the doorway, watching him, wondering what was going through his mind.

It was only when she shifted her weight slightly that he turned, his eyes locking onto hers with a sharpness that took her breath away.

"Ms. Hartwell," he said, his voice as cold and controlled as ever. "I wasn't expecting you."

"I was just on my way to the kitchen," Emily said, her

voice as steady as she could muster. "I didn't mean to intrude."

Devlin's gaze flicked over her, his eyes narrowing ever so slightly. He didn't move toward her, but there was a definite shift in his posture. A subtle tightening, as if he were bracing himself.

"You never intrude." His voice was almost a whisper. "But there's no need to lurk. Come in."

Emily hesitated for just a moment before stepping into the room, her eyes never leaving his. She couldn't shake the feeling that she was walking toward the edge of the cliff. It was full, heavy, like swollen storm clouds before the first crack of thunder.

"I'm sorry for what happened yesterday," Devlin continued, his words coming out unexpectedly. He took a slow step toward her, his expression unreadable. "I didn't mean to... snap."

Emily blinked, taken aback. She had expected him to stay distant, to hide behind his walls, not apologize for anything. But here he was, standing in front of her, acknowledging his behavior even if in just a small way.

"You don't need to apologize," Emily said, her voice soft but firm. "I understand."

He let out a breath, the tension in his shoulders easing just a little. "Maybe. But I don't want to make things difficult between us. I am your employer, and you're entitled to safety. It is my job to provide that, a duty of care if you will."

Emily studied him. There was something odd about

the way he spoke of safety, a subtle shift in tone that felt contradictory to the employer-employee boundary he was trying to reinforce. It intrigued her. No one had ever cared much for her safety before, not in any meaningful way at least. It made her feel warm inside, a surprising feeling coming from the man in front of her.

He was a walking contradiction. Cold and distant one moment, humble and almost protective the next. He seemed lost—lost in his past, lost in the legacy that haunted him. Her fingers ached to brush at the wisps of hair that fell across his forehead, to bring some tenderness into his life. She wondered how long it had been since he'd been touched in such a way, with no ulterior motives or demands.

She knew what she was doing was dangerous, that she was walking a line she shouldn't cross. But she couldn't stop herself. Every moment she spent with him, every quiet exchange, made her want to know more.

"Devlin," she whispered, and for the first time, she used his name instead of his title. "Why did you hire me?"

He froze, the words catching him off guard. His dark eyes flicked down to the floor. He said nothing for a long time, only cleared his throat and stared at their feet. When he finally raised his eyes to hers and spoke, his voice was gravelly, much like it had been the first time she'd met him.

"Because I needed someone. Someone who wouldn't run from the things I can't face."

The honesty in his voice startled her. There was

vulnerability there, barely a hint, but it was there. The sound of whooshing blood roared in her ears, and her throat felt tight. She could hear her heartbeat pounding in her own head. Butterflies danced in her belly.

She wanted him to come to her. Or if she could only find the courage, she could go to him, close the distance between them and feel their bodies pressing against one another. Her body was hot with nervous desire. He was a candle blazing hot and bright in front of her, and the only thing she wanted was to be enveloped by his flame.

"Why don't you let anyone close?" Emily asked, her voice barely above a whisper. The question had been on the tip of her tongue for days now, and she needed an answer. She needed to know.

Devlin's expression hardened. "It's better that way. Safer."

Emily's chest tightened. Safety again. Who had he tried to protect? And how had he failed them? She knew there was more to his past than he let on, but hearing him say it out loud made it all the more real. Suddenly, she felt more like a true-crime detective than anything she'd trained for. There was real danger in his life, and Emily wondered if she should be afraid of him after all.

"What are you trying to protect people from?" she asked, but what they both knew she was really asking was, "What are you trying to protect me from?"

Devlin didn't answer right away. Instead, he took a step toward her, then another and another until he was so close she could feel the heat of his body, smell his scent—wood, leather, the sharpness of liquor on his breath.

"Me," he growled.

Emily's breath hitched, and a ball of heat exploded from the center of her most sensitive parts. Devlin's hand inched away from his side, as if he wanted to reach for her, but he stopped himself. She stared at the hand he'd balled into a fist and licked her lips, wondering at what it would feel like to have those hands gripping her with such force that the tips dug into her skin and his knuckles turned white.

She found herself leaning toward him, her body pulled in ever so slightly. She dragged her eyes away from his hand and found him staring at her with such hunger that her mouth went dry. She felt like prey finally captured, only there was nothing she wanted more than to be devoured.

Part of her hoped his control would finally snap, that he would grab her and take what they both wanted so desperately. Because she couldn't bring herself to cross that line. But he remained in control, as always. He jerked away, his hands clenched tightly against his sides as he stepped back.

"Enough," he said, his voice flat and emotionless. "Go. Now."

Emily simply stood there staring at him, her heart pounding in her chest. She wanted more. She wanted him to let her in, to open up to her. She wanted to know what it felt like to be enveloped by his heat, to know what was between them. Instead, she felt foolish and rejected.

Tears pricked at her eyes, but pride had her stiffening her back. Her eyes flashed. Her voice filled with an intensity of her own, anger barely contained, and she spoke in such a way that every syllable was enunciated. "Do not speak to me like that ever again."

And then she did go.

She turned on her heel and marched out of the room, and she didn't let herself cry until she was safely tucked in her own bed.

7

The evening at Moore Manor was always quiet, but tonight was different. The usual stillness of the mansion was replaced with an anger, her anger. She'd spent most of the day in other parts of the house, but as usual, the library pulled at her, and she'd ended her day here. She pushed through the books and dust, the usual rhythm of her work more disjointed than before, but she couldn't focus. Her thoughts kept drifting back to Devlin.

Their last interaction left so much unspoken. Desire, vulnerability, rejection, anger. All of it roiled around inside of her, loose threads of molten metal burning everything they touched. She looked around the room, at all the secrets she'd uncovered and those yet to be revealed. Yet, today she had little patience for them.

When she reached for another book, her fingers brushed against another family album. She paused, her pulse quickening. The album was old, its cover worn with age, and for a moment, she hesitated. She hadn't meant to get drawn into these family relics again, but there they were every time she turned around.

She shouldn't pry, should continue to respect the privacy Devlin had asked for. But in the end, anger won out, and she found she didn't care as much. It was wrong. She knew it as she sat down with the album, as she flipped through pages of black-and-white photographs one by one.

She didn't care.

Looking at the faces of his ancestors, she noted how alike they all looked. Even Devlin, generations removed from the people in these pictures, bore a striking resemblance to them. She thought about the pictures she'd seen of him as a younger boy. He had been different once— more innocent, less burdened by the weight of the world. But that boy was long gone, replaced by an insufferable, arrogant man who toyed with her like a cat batting around a mouse it probably didn't ever really intend to eat, anyway.

Yet, as much as she told herself to stop this madness, quit this godforsaken job that wasn't worth the chaos it was creating in her mind, she couldn't bring herself to do it. She couldn't help wondering what had happened to him. What had turned him into the brooding man who now haunted these halls?

A voice niggled at the back of her mind with a warning. This wasn't a mystery that was hers to solve. He wasn't a man that was hers to fix. Emily shook off the thoughts. She wasn't trying to fix anything, she told herself.

The clock on the wall chimed, and she blinked. She glanced at the clock, and the room suddenly felt far dimmer. It was late, later than she'd intended to stay. She closed the album and tucked it back onto the shelf. Slinging her bag over her shoulder, she headed toward the door. Her phone buzzed in her pocket, and she wiggled it out of her pocket as she walked.

It was a text from Zoe.

Zoe:

> You still at work? Thought we were going to grab dinner tonight.

Emily glanced at the time again and groaned. Not only had she let the day slip into evening, but she'd also apparently forgotten about dinner plans, too.

Emily:

> I lost track of time.
>
> Finishing up!!!
>
> I'll be home soon, I promise!

She hit send, but she halted mid-step and stared at her phone. Not that she didn't want to spend time with Zoe— it was just that suddenly she didn't actually want to leave. It was a strange feeling to have, especially amid a whole mess of unresolved fury. The more she got wrapped up in the house, in Devlin, the harder it was becoming to separate the two worlds. She wasn't sure how she felt about that.

A moment later, Zoe replied.

Zoe:

> Uh-huh. You keep this up, and I'm going to have to start calling you a workaholic. Seriously, Em, what's keeping you?

Emily:

> It's... complicated. I'll explain when I get back. Promise.

Zoe:

> Fine, but you owe me a drink and dinner next time. You're buying.

> For making me look like an ass at this place.

Emily closed her eyes and cringed. She didn't realize Zoe was already at the restaurant. Her guilt magnified, but she would make it up to Zoe. Taking a deep breath, she tucked her phone back in her pocket. There was comfort in knowing she could be human and royally fuck shit up, but her friend would still love her all the same. She had some ass to kiss, of course, but the love was always there. It also helped to know Zoe would not let her slip away into this strange, isolated world without at least a little push-back. Even if her friend had to physically drag her out by the hair. Zoe would do it; she was sure of that.

Still, maybe missing dinner tonight was for the best, she thought as she started walking again. The last thing she wanted was to keep Zoe in the dark, but tonight, she wasn't sure how to explain the storm of emotions swirling inside her. She was confused, if she was being honest with herself. The more time she spent with Devlin, the more she wanted to know. Despite the fact that he was an emotionally volatile asshole, of course. Or maybe in spite of it? She didn't care to speculate—she probably wouldn't like the answer, anyway.

The sound of her own footsteps echoing down the hallway was grounding, as was the rhythm of the vibrations that reverberated up her body with every step. As she walked, her eyes caught on the familiar sight of the study where Devlin usually retreated to when he wanted to be alone.

Tonight, the door was open. A sliver of light spilled out from the crack, and she could see the faint outline of his figure through the doorway. He stood so that she only saw his profile from the side, though there was no mistaking the stiff and unyielding posture. He was perfectly still, looking out the window.

The urge to approach him was undeniable. Emily had learned over the past few weeks that when Devlin stood like that, when he didn't acknowledge her presence right away, it was because he was lost in thought. Lost in whatever burden he carried around in silence.

But all the emotions she'd carefully tucked into a box in her mind were suddenly restless, beating and pushing against the wood that contained them. Now that he was right in front of her, she wasn't sure she wanted to keep them locked away.

She paused in the hallway, not yet sure if she would continue walking away or if she would approach him. He acted as if he didn't see her, but she knew better. Devlin always knew when she was near, just as she could sense him. It was as infuriating as it was intoxicating.

Devlin didn't speak at first, and Emily wasn't sure if she should wait for him to acknowledge her or simply leave. She didn't know what she needed to hear from him, nor was she certain she was even ready for whatever he might be prepared to say. She pulled her shoulders back and raised her chin.

Finally, Devlin turned to face her fully. His eyes met hers, dark and unreadable. "It's time you took some time off. Paid, of course," he said. His tone was, as usual, firm and direct, but it was softer than usual.

Emily blinked, surprised. "Time off?" she echoed, raising an eyebrow. "That's not exactly the apology I had in mind."

Devlin raised a brow in return, the faintest trace of something human slipping through the usual veneer of control. His posture shifted slightly, relaxing. "You won't get one. I won't apologize for the kind of man I am."

"Oh, really? And what kind of man is that?"

"The kind you shouldn't want to get close to." Though as he said it, he took a step closer to her as if in challenge.

"And what if I do?" She licked her lips.

"Hmmm." He made the noise in his throat, letting her question hang in the air unanswered. "I've been thinking that a little change of scenery would be good for both of us."

Emily knew what he was doing, but she allowed him to change the subject, her curiosity stronger than her need for resolution. She wasn't sure where this was coming from or where he wanted it to go, but the sudden invitation felt like another shift, one that she wasn't quite prepared for. "What do you have in mind?"

He stepped closer again, and even though he was still half a room away from her, his presence was overwhelming. His gaze locked with hers, and the ache in her chest that had become so familiar flared to life.

"I know a place—a restaurant. It's a favorite of mine. You'll join me for dinner tomorrow evening."

The words hung in the air, heavy and deliberate. Emily's heart skipped a beat, her mind racing. It coming on the tail end of a non-apology raised her hackles, but yet again curiosity won out.

"You're inviting me to dinner?" she repeated.

"It was not a request."

"Oh, thank you for clarifying," she said, propping a hand on her hip and tucking her tongue into her cheek. She sniffed and raised her nose in her air, pursing her lips. "I'm not sure I'm available."

Devlin didn't flinch at her attitude. It seemed to amuse him, in fact, and his eyes remained steady and unyielding as he looked at her. "It's time for us to get to know each other outside of this house."

Despite her commitment to hating him at that moment, she couldn't ignore the pull. There was something exciting about the way he issued orders, as frustrating as that was. They certainly needed to set some boundaries, but power could be fun to play with. More than the allure of that, it was clear that he wanted her company. He wanted to take her out of the confines of the manor and into his world—if only for one night. The thought was... tempting. Dangerous, but tempting.

She swallowed, thinking back to what she knew of the women who'd come before her. "And what do you expect in return?"

Devlin's lips twitched, the briefest of smiles crossing his face, as if he knew exactly where her thoughts had gone. "You. Nothing more."

That didn't even come close to answering her question. Emily felt a flutter in her stomach, a mix of excitement and anxiety. "I'll think about it," she said with a lazy shrug.

Devlin smirked. "A dress will arrive for you by five. Be ready at seven o'clock. I'll pick you up."

With that he brushed past her, leaving Emily standing alone with a racing heart and thoughts that were a whirl of uncertainty. Just like that, she was going on a date with Devlin Moore.

Tomorrow night.

Dinner.

And whatever that would lead to.

8

———

The restaurant was everything Devlin had promised. It was sleek and polished, with an air of quiet exclusivity that made Emily feel both out of place and thrilled by it. Soft golden lights cast long shadows across the tables, the atmosphere both intimate and distant. It was the kind of place where you didn't just eat; you experienced the food, the ambiance, the company.

Tonight, that company was Devlin Moore, and he looked every bit as dangerous as she'd been warned. He'd parted and combed his hair back over, slicking the pieces that habitually fell on his forehead at the temple ever so slightly. A white dress shirt, black pants, and a black vest were perfectly tailored to his body. He wore no jacket, accessorizing with only a black tie and a thin chain that draped from one button into a small pocket on the front of the vest.

Emily brushed at the subtle ruching down the midsection of the black velvet dress he'd picked out for her. True to his word, it had arrived before five pm that day, and it fit like a glove. She wasn't sure how he'd known her measurements so well, nor how he had gotten a tailored dress to her so quickly, but she was sure she didn't want to know.

"Stop it," he said into her ear as she pulled at the hem.

"It's too short," she hissed.

He leaned behind her, taking his time to look her up and down from head to toe. Facing her again, he said, "No, it's not."

Emily rolled her eyes and yanked down the hem again. He grabbed her hand without looking at her, tucking it into the crook of his arm as a server led them to what had to be the best table in the restaurant. It was tucked away in a corner by the windows, the city lights twinkling like distant stars just beyond the glass.

The evening was a beautifully crafted experience, but despite his assurances to the contrary, she couldn't shake the feeling that he was expecting something from her. She had to admit a part of her wouldn't mind giving it to him. It wasn't a part of herself she could indulge in. She'd come to terms with that, and she was grateful for Devlin's control when she would've given in.

He was right. He was her employer, and he owed her a safe working environment. Indulging in any intimacy would compromise that. Nevermind that they'd already done that to some extent. The past couldn't change, but she had every right to alter the trajectory of the future.

Tonight, they would have a professional dinner, nothing more.

Emily noted Devlin was quieter than usual tonight, more aloof, and she wondered if he had come to the same conclusions as she. Though he was constantly watching her, studying her, adjusting his body according to her movements. She attributed it to a more intentional focus on her care. He was a gentleman, after all.

"So," Emily began, breaking the silence, her voice light. "What exactly does your family empire consist of? You've never really said."

She half expected him to shut down, but he seemed amused, one corner of his mouth lifting in a small grin. He leaned back in his chair. "Many things, actually. I dabble here and there. It's not something I'm usually asked about," he said pointedly. He took a sip of his wine, the way his fingers looked curling around the glass setting her mouth to watering despite her decision not to indulge in such fantasies anymore. "But it's... vast."

His amusement intrigued Emily, but it didn't escape her notice that his answer was evasive. "What kind of business are we talking about, Devlin?" she pressed, unable to hide the curiosity in her voice.

He met her gaze briefly, his expression hardening, but instead of answering, he changed the subject. "Let's not talk about business tonight, Emily," he said, his voice softer now, but the edge was still there. "Let's just... enjoy dinner."

Emily felt a flicker of frustration, but she knew better than to push too hard. Devlin was a man of secrets, of layers, and she knew if she dug deep enough, she would uncover them eventually. She was patient. She could wait.

She settled back in her chair, her lips curling into a teasing smile. "You know, I think you'd be better at talking about yourself if you weren't so secretive all the time."

Devlin smirked at her, but there was a shadow behind his smile, something dark and possessive. "You don't know anything about me yet, Emily. But you will. In time."

She tilted her head slightly, intrigued despite herself. "Is that so?" she asked. He was wrong. She would finish this job eventually and move on to the next. They didn't live in the same worlds, so when that happened—and it would—they would never see each other again. He would live forever in her memory as that one hot boss she knew better than to date.

Devlin nodded and made a sound of agreement. "In the meantime, I'll just enjoy your company tonight."

The conversation flowed easily from topic to topic, each word exchanged lighter than the last. They spoke of the music they liked—she listened to pop while his tastes unsurprisingly ran darker—and movies they'd deemed exciting enough to see in theaters. Their tastes seemed so opposite to one another in so many ways, but there were a surprising number of interests and values they shared. Both of them were committed to their families. They shared a love of books and reading. They even shared a love of the outdoors, an interesting fact that made them both chuckle considering how much time recently they had spent in the manor.

Despite the ease of conversation, there was a constant undercurrent to it, a steady pull beneath the surface that neither of them was willing to acknowledge. When they finally left the restaurant, it was everything Emily could do to hold fast to her resolve not to let this go any further. They'd laughed, flirted, taken one look at each other's plates and agreed to try everything. If it were anyone else, she'd be opening her calendar and scheduling a second date on the spot.

But this was Devlin Moore, and he wasn't just anyone.

He was her boss for one, but he was also a walking red flag. Death, family secrets, an empire of wealth he refused to discuss. Then there was the way she'd been warned about him. No, he was not a man to trifle with, however casually. Especially casually.

As they arrived back at her apartment, Emily toyed with a curl in her side-swept hair. How bittersweet the night had been—beautiful but temporal. Now she knew how Cinderella had felt, always knowing the ball would end at midnight, and she would go back to her normal life. Emily sighed. This was her midnight, she thought as Devlin parked the car.

"Stay," he said, placing his hand firmly on her thigh. Then he was sliding out of the car and walking around the hood. He opened the door for her, offering his hand as she stepped out.

Her cheeks flushed, and she was sure the smile on her face was probably the goofiest of her life, but she couldn't help it. Tonight, she was a princess. However reluctantly.

When she was about to say goodbye, Devlin insisted on walking her to her door. Again, he tucked her hand into the crook of his elbow as they walked. If it wasn't already before, the electricity between them was almost unbearable now.

When they reached her door, Emily turned to face him, her pulse racing as she looked up at him. The tension was at its peak, and she could feel the heat of his body so close to hers, feel the breath catch in his throat as his hand lingered near her waist.

"Thank you for tonight," she said, her voice robbed of its strength as she used all of her reserves to resist the temptation to invite him inside. "It was a lovely way to reset our working relationship."

"Is that what we did?" he asked.

Emily couldn't be sure, but she could've sworn he'd pulled her body closer to his. She put her hands on his chest, the linen of his vest smooth and cool beneath her fingertips. She meant to push him away, but she found her hands lingering there. Squeezing her eyes closed with a sigh, she nodded and made to pull her hands away.

He caught her wrists, pinning her hands to him. "I don't think so."

"I don't understand."

"I think you do." Devlin's gaze flicked to her lips, his body rigid with desire. He pulled her flush to him, and his breath was warm on her face. "You understand exactly."

"We can't. This is a bad idea. I... we... You—" she stuttered as his lips trailed down her neck and she felt his teeth sink into the tender flesh there. He wasn't gentle either. She gasped, a sharp sound that ended in a breathy moan. His cock was hard and pressed into her belly. She felt him throb against her as his mouth worked at her neck.

He raked his teeth up her neck to whisper in her ear, his voice husky, "I think I've made it clear what I want."

Warning bells sounded in Emily's mind, her thoughts screaming with all the reasons this couldn't happen. When she finally managed to dislodge herself from him, if only by a few inches, she looked up at him and shook her head.

"No," she breathed. "You can't have it."

He looked shocked, almost offended by the notion that she would say no. "I can't," he repeated, every sound of the word pronounced with intention.

Before she could respond, he yanked her against him hard enough that he knocked the breath out of her. His lips crashed down on hers in a kiss that showed her just how hungry he was. Emily gasped, but his mouth swallowed the sound, and she found herself pulled into the spell he was weaving.

Hands that had tried to push him away now gripped the fabric of his vest as if she were drowning and he was the lifejacket. Her heart pounded as his fingertips dug into her hips so hard they were sure to leave bruises. He shoved her against the wall, his body never leaving contact with hers, and ground his hips into hers at a pace that matched that of his mouth.

"I can't have what I want?" he taunted her, his mouth

moving down her body until he was biting hard into the flesh at her breast. He yanked down the material to expose her nipple, taking it between his teeth as his hand continued its journey down her body, down her thigh, back up between her legs.

He rubbed his palm over her underwear, growling at the wet heat he found there. Emily's breath caught, and she moaned, pressing herself against his hand, desperate for more. That they were still outside her apartment, heaving against one another on the wall by the entryway, was long forgotten. The world had melted away in a pool of desire at their feet.

"Tell me I can have what I want," he ordered her, her fingers circling her clit in an ever increasing rhythm as she writhed against him. "Tell me."

"You can have it!" she cried.

Not done torturing her yet, he knelt before her and snaked an arm around her thigh, a finger coming to rest at the entrance of her ass. He clamped his mouth over her clit, the thin fabric of her underwear still a barrier between them.

"Beg for it," he said, his voice a low groan against her.

Her hands dug into his hair. She couldn't help but push her pussy into his face, and she begged. "Oh, fuck, Devlin. Please, please take it. Take whatever you want. Take it all."

"Good girl," he growled into her pussy as he pushed her underwear to the side and at last clamped his mouth over her clit, the flat of his tongue pressing and rubbing against her rhythmically. His fingers dove into her wet heat, while with his other hand he pressed a finger into her ass. She gasped and froze, her entire body paralyzed by all the sensations.

Everything—every doubt, every hesitation—disappeared in an instant. There was an animal in him, a dark hunger that threatened to swallow her light even as it pined for it. She could feel his control slipping as the desire between them built to a fever pitch, feel the raw intensity in him. In that moment, she knew he could not hold back much longer; he was a man on the edge.

Pleasure built in her, bringing her closer and closer to that delicious explosion, and to the decision she would ultimately have to make if she let this continue: whether she was willing to be pulled over the edge with him.

But before she could reach either precipice, Devlin pulled away with a growl, his chest heaving as he stepped back. His eyes were dark and filled with conflicting emotions she couldn't interpret. Her breathing was ragged, and she was suddenly very aware of how exposed they were. Nervously, Emily pulled her clothing into place, her eyes glued to his.

He reached out and gripped her chin between his fingers. For a moment, she thought he was going to kiss her. Instead, he said, "You're mine now."

Without another word, he turned on his heel and stormed away, leaving Emily standing with her arms held limply at her sides, brows drawn together, wondering how someone could so thoroughly claim her and yet seem so angry about it.

She stood motionless on the front stoop of her apartment. Her chest rose and fell like the beat of a hummingbird's wings, a flush of arousal still bright upon her cheeks. For longer than she'd ever dare to admit, she stared out into the night where he'd disappeared.

She didn't know what had just happened, but she knew one thing for sure: Devlin Moore was every bit as dangerous as he was reputed to be.

Only she wasn't sure whether he was more dangerous to his enemies or to her heart.

9
———

Devlin sat behind his desk, his fingers drumming absently against the polished wood. The mountain of paperwork in front of him was endless, but his attention was elsewhere, as it often was these days. His thoughts drifted back to Emily, her presence in the house, her every word, every glance. She was there, and yet she wasn't, always lingering in the background of his mind like a shadow he couldn't shake.

He had to stay focused. He had to push it aside.

But the longer Emily stayed at Moore Manor, the harder it became to pretend she wasn't affecting him. She had wormed her way into his every thought, into his very body, and it was driving him insane. The desire to claim her, the unrelenting need to protect her, was too much. He could barely function.

"Mr. Moore?"

His attention snapped back to reality, and he glanced

up. Kara stood in the doorway of his office, a file in her hands. His assistant, ever-efficient, ever-astute. She knew him better than anyone else, and right now, that was a problem.

Kara wasn't blind to the way things had been going lately. She could see right through his attempts to stay detached from Emily, and she would know something had happened the second he began talking. She may not know exactly what had transpired, but she wouldn't need a play-by-play to put the basics together.

To her credit, she never pushed. She just watched, observing and collecting data, as always. Silent until her opinion was louder than her willpower, and even then it was usually in Devlin's best interest to hear her out. It was infuriating, but she was rarely wrong.

"You have an update for me?" Devlin asked, his voice clipped, trying to maintain his composure and betray as little of his thoughts as possible.

Kara stepped into the room, closing the door behind her, her heels clicking softly against the floor. "The shipments are on schedule. But we've had some issues with the... logistics. There's a potential problem at the eastern port. I've spoken with our contact, and he assures me he'll get it smoothed over, but it's going to take some time."

"How much? Time is the one thing we don't have, and we can't afford any more delays." Devlin's jaw tensed as he went over various scenarios and solutions in his head.

Kara nodded and moved closer, placing the file on the

desk. "Of course. But it's not just that. There's also the matter of the latest round of negotiations with the twins."

His eyes darkened immediately, a shadow passing across his face. "Those two again? I thought we were done with them. They're too reckless. They want the respect their father commanded but want to do nothing to maintain it."

Kara cleared her throat, hesitating. "About that... They have asked that you be informed that they politely decline your offer to terminate the contract."

"What?" Devlin's voice was cold and flat.

She cringed and continued. "They've also requested to move up the pickup date by two weeks." Devlin swore. "Mr. Moore, to be perfectly frank, this isn't sustainable."

"I had no idea," he said, sarcasm dripping from his tongue like honey off a warm spoon. Kara was unaffected and simply cocked her head and raised a brow at his tone. He groaned and scrubbed his hands over his face. "Sorry," he said, his voice muffled by his hands.

"What do you want to do?"

"Set up a meeting with the twins. No weapons, no assistants, no friends. Only them. I'll explain to them in no uncertain terms that when I terminate a contract, it is not a negotiation. They will either understand or be terminated themselves."

Kara nodded, making a note to make the call from their secure line. "What about the problem at the port?"

"I'll handle it." He glanced down and tapped a few keys on his laptop, bringing up his calendar. Checking the watch he wore on his left wrist, he noted the time and whispered under his breath as he did the math. "I've got time to squeeze in a surprise visit today and sort it out. In the meantime, make sure the port stays clear. If anyone gets too curious, they disappear. Understand?"

Kara's expression didn't waver. "Yes, sir."

Devlin let out a breath, his mind racing, eyes drawn to a portrait of his father on the far wall. "Sometimes I curse him for leaving me with all this."

"I know," Kara said, her voice soft and compassionate.

"Some days I want to disappear." His head drooped, and Kara said nothing. Then a shadow passed over his face, and his fingers clenched into fists, the skin stretching white over his knuckles. "Other days I want to make them disappear."

"You're not untouchable," she said, her voice quiet but firm.

"I don't want to be."

Kara inhaled sharply but remained silent. He wondered if she did so out of concern or fear. Or maybe she knew him well enough to know his volatile moods, how he was as confident in himself as he was self-loathing, how quickly he could go from one to another. He didn't care. He was who he was.

Devlin turned away from her, staring out the window. The darkness outside mirrored the thoughts swirling in his head. "I'll be leaving within the hour for the dock. Make sure this stays under the radar."

Kara hesitated for a moment. "Just don't forget what happened before."

Devlin's jaw tightened. She didn't say Sophia's name, but it hung in the air unspoken but understood, draping over them like a heavy death shroud. "I don't need to be reminded of my failures."

"You didn't fail her. Your sister—" Kara stopped mid-sentence when he raised a hand to silence her, shaking his head with a warning look in his eyes. She knew better than to ignore him. Deep as their relationship was, she had no illusions about the kind of man he was.

Or what he was capable of when crossed.

Not that he would ever harm her. Others? Without hesitation. Her? Never. She was too important to him, too valuable, and she made sure she was always the person who knew too much to be disposable. Kara Voss wasn't an idiot or very sentimental for that matter. She knew her place, and she enjoyed the comfortable life her position with the Moore family provided her. Her friendship, if you could call it that, with Devlin was a perk, a bonus. It was nice to care about the person who employed you, especially in her line of work.

It was because she cared she spoke again, albeit with slow precision and a soft tone. "You don't have to keep doing this. This isn't a legacy, and you owe him nothing."

"Hmm," he said, the sound more of a drawn out hum in the back of his throat than an actual response. Kara glanced at the old portrait and then back at him, a look of unease flashing across her face. She was worried she'd gone too far, pushed too much.

Maybe, he admitted to himself. He considered her words, how he felt about them. He didn't need to be reminded of his sister or of his commitment to a family legacy that was destroying them. Because she was wrong. He did owe his father, his family. His wealth, power, social position, access, all of it and more was because of his father and his father before him and his father before him.

Generation after generation, they had built themselves up from nothing, each expected to continue that legacy, by whatever means necessary. They knew they would have to—be expected to, even—make sacrifices. So, his parents were dead; Sophia was dead. Because of his choices, his mistakes. He had failed her. He had failed his family.

And there was no going back. What was there to go back to? This was all he'd ever known. He couldn't undo the past; now, he was the only one left. If he let it fall to ruin, then what was it all for—all the pain and sacrifice and death? And if he turned away from that legacy, tucked tail and ran to save himself... he may survive, but he'd forever be remembered as the man who let the empire fall.

He was too proud for that.

"But I do. I owe him everything, so I can't stop. Not now," he said, his voice a hollow whisper.

"Can't... or won't?" Kara cocked her head to the side.

"It doesn't matter." Stiffening his shoulders, Devlin turned his attention to his shift cuff, fidgeting with it until the button was redone. "Did you have anything else to add? My patience is thin."

Kara shook her head, her face void of emotion. She held her notebook to her chest. "I'll take care of everything. Be careful."

Devlin flashed a humorless grin that seemed more like that of a predator about to pounce on its prey than a man smiling. "I've got it under control."

Kara nodded and made to leave the room. When she reached the door, she turned back, and her eyes softened and lingered on him as he stared at his father's portrait. There was a look in her eyes, the weight of emotion behind them, but she sighed quietly, and a mask of professionalism fell over her face.

"Will there be anything else, Mr. Moore?" she asked.

"No." Devlin waved her away, his gaze locked on his father's. He didn't hear her leave the room, but then the door clicked softly, and he knew he was alone again.

He stood lost in the silence. The weight of the conversation, of the loss of his parents and of his sister's death, hung over him like a cloud that refused to disperse. There was nothing to be done. Not after everything he'd built, everything he'd sacrificed for this.

His mind drifted back to Emily. She was still here, still in the house, still pulling at him in ways he couldn't explain. Devlin wanted her with a feral, desperate hunger. He was hard just thinking about the feel of her under his body, the way she'd responded to his touch. It would be all too easy to march down the hall right now, rip her clothes from her body, and fuck her senseless where she stood. He didn't care if she was ready, if the invasion of his cock left her delicious pussy raw and bruised. In fact, that only increased the allure. Let her leave the house throbbing. Let her leave with the memory that she belonged only to him.

He groaned and adjusted his trousers. He had to think of something, anything, else. There was work to be done, and he couldn't afford for a woman he couldn't even have to become a distraction that interfered with what needed to be done.

Because for some infernal reason what he felt for her was more than physical desire. He wanted to claim her, to make her his and only his, to hide her away from the world and all its dangers.

He couldn't have her because he couldn't afford to lose her.

If something were to happen to her, he'd have no choice but to burn the world down and himself with it. The heart could only bear so much sadness before it was too heavy to beat.

He tried to push her from his mind, forget the taste of her that lingered on his lips or how soft her skin was under his hands, and reminded himself that she was off limits, the mouthwatering slice of cake he couldn't bite into if he wanted to avoid the pain that came with eating it.

Too bad for both of them, he liked pain.

～

EMILY WALKED down the hall with a hand pressed into the small of her back. She sighed at the ache that had taken up residence there and tried not to think of the burning between her shoulder blades.

She was ready to call it quits for the day, and she didn't really care that it was early. Let Devlin complain if he was so inclined. After what she'd dealt with following their evening out, he was lucky she hadn't quit on the spot.

She was nearly to Devlin's office when the faint sound of voices caught her attention. She didn't mean to eavesdrop—she didn't even want to—but once again her curiosity got the better of her. And honestly, the man's body parts had been in every orifice in her body at this point, she thought with a slight blush; she was entitled to learn something about him. If she had to eavesdrop to get some answers... well, that was his own damn fault.

At first, she thought the voices inside must be discussing business. It was the easiest assumption considering what room it was and how much time Devlin spent there. Though as the words came into focus, she found herself second-guessing that assumption.

"... There's also the matter of the latest round of negotiations with the twins." Kara's voice drifted through the crack in the door.

Emily's breath caught in her throat. She could hear the tension in Kara's voice, and despite her better instincts, she slowed and strained to listen. She heard them having a muffled conversation, and then Devlin spoke again.

"I'll handle it," he said.

Emily's heart raced. She didn't know exactly what they were talking about, but it sounded dangerous? Was she overreacting? There wasn't anything particularly sinister so far, but something in his tone sounded severe. She should have walked away, should have left and pretended she had heard nothing, but her feet rooted to the floor. The conversation pulled her in deeper.

She thought she heard more talking, lower now, and Devlin's voice followed, firm and cold. "If anyone gets too curious, they disappear. Understand?"

A shiver snaked down Emily's spine. She stepped back, her thoughts a whirlwind of chaotic screaming and wailing sirens. Whatever she thought she would overhear, this was wildly different. Devlin Moore wasn't just a successful businessman, a man born to a family fortune living in a dilapidated mansion. No, he was dangerous and involved in something equally so, not to mention illegal from the sound of it.

So why did that make him more alluring?

Stupid, stupid girl, she chided herself. Her heart pounded in her chest as she turned away from the door and hurried to the front door. The weight of the conversation settled over her like a storm cloud. She didn't know what to make of it, but one thing was clear: getting involved with Devlin Moore was not just risky. It was life-threatening.

But even as she tried to push the thoughts away, a part of her—the part that rooted for every anti-hero, villain, and vampire to end up with the girl—wanted more.

10

———

The air outside smelled of moss and sun-warmed stone.

Emily stepped onto the worn flagstone path, grateful for the stretch of open space and light. She didn't mean to find the gardens secreted away at the back of the property. She'd merely followed her feet and ended up here, though she wasn't disappointed or upset about that in the slightest.

The gardens at the back of Moore Manor were sprawling, the kind of space that had once been grand but now teetered between cultivated and overgrown, like a memory that hadn't yet faded entirely.

Wild roses clung to ancient trellises. Ferns crept out from shady corners. Marble statues—some cracked, some moss-covered—stood sentry in small alcoves. It was enchanting in a way that made her feel like she'd stepped into someone else's dream.

She walked slowly, letting the sun soak into her skin. After hours of working in the dark recesses of the house, where the air was thick with dust and time, she needed anything but quiet. She needed sunlight and life and fresh air. Her back ached, and a strange substance stained her fingers—whatever had been used to polish a collection of small brass statues shoved into a corner of the parlor. There was a smear of something suspicious on her shirt she didn't want to think about.

She found a low stone wall near the hydrangeas and sat, tilting her face to the sun. The blue of the sky filtered through the lacework of branches above, dappling the overgrown path with shattered rays of light.

So engrossed in her basking was Emily that she didn't hear him until he spoke.

"It appears the gardens have a visitor today."

She jerked, her breath catching in her throat. She turned to find Devlin standing a few feet away looking devilishly handsome, as always, and an odd mix of tense and relaxed.

He wasn't in a suit today—just a black button-down with the sleeves rolled up and dark slacks. His hair was disheveled, as it often was, like he'd run a frustrated hand through it a dozen times, and there was a stiffness in his shoulders.

Emily eyed him, her mind unsure whether to respond to him positively or negatively. "How did you know I was all the way out here?"

"I have my ways." He moved his shoulders and

smirked. It didn't feel wrong to see him so playful, but the change in him was still mildly unnerving, especially considering the conversation she'd overheard only days before.

"Technically, I'm on break. I promise not to uproot anything."

He stepped closer, hands in his pockets, gaze scanning the flowerbeds. "How did you find it? Most people don't realize it's back here. Or don't care."

She shrugged, looking out into the expanse of greenery and blooms. Looking at anything but him. "I don't know that I did. I just followed the walking path until it found me."

"You're the first to come out here in years," he said, his voice low and somber. "Well, besides me."

"It's beautiful," she said. "Do you come here often?"

His eyes flicked to hers, and he shook his head. "It was my mother's favorite place."

A moment of silence passed where neither of them spoke, the air heavy with the weight of what should've been such a simple statement. She wanted to say something, add to the conversation in some way, but she didn't know much about mothers. Growing up without one tended to make someone less than an expert on the whole experience.

"She used to bring us out here when we were kids," he said finally. "I think she liked that it didn't look perfect. That it was a little wild."

Emily's expression softened. The direction of the

conversation surprised her as much as the tenderness in his voice.

"Let me show you mine." He stood and held out a hand to her. It was not a request or an order but something in between.

"Your what?"

"My favorite place."

She wanted to hesitate. She should have, but she had no choice but to take his hand and wordlessly allow him to lead her.

He guided her down a winding path edged by rose-bushes growing wild and scraggly. Petals scattered underfoot like confetti. Sunlight dappled the stone beneath their feet, and tiny flecks of quartz in it sparkled like miniature diamonds. The scent of damp earth and fading flowers curled into the air.

Devlin was quiet as they walked. His posture was more relaxed than she'd seen him lately, but his movements seemed stilted and foreign, not the picture of suave charm she was used to. It was as if the silence made him uncomfortable, but words would cost too much.

They reached a narrow clearing beneath an arch of ivy-draped iron. A stone bench sat beside a tiny pond, the water still and dark, and lilies drifted on the surface like sleeping stars. Devlin led her to a part of the wall tucked behind the bench. He let go of her hand long enough to part the ivy, and she saw it: a wooden door with large black iron fittings.

Emily gasped. "It's like something out of a fairy tale."

Devlin's smile was faint, almost wistful. "Just wait."

He pulled a black key out of his pocket and pushed it into the lock. It groaned loudly as he turned it, giving way eventually and allowing the door to swing open. Devlin held the ivy up so she could duck underneath.

Inside, Emily turned in a slow circle, soaking in every sight and sound and sensation inside this secret place. A wide grin spread across her face at the wild abundance around her. Ivy grew over winding brambles, flowers exploded everywhere, birds flitted from branch to branch, and she could hear the sounds of tiny critters shuffling around in the leaf litter.

"I used to come here when I wanted to disappear," he said.

She looked at him, surprised by the honesty in his tone.

"Sometimes I still do," he added.

"You're not very good at hiding."

"I used to be."

He took her hands once more and drew her to a wooden bench that sat under the branches of a dogwood tree. He kept her hands in his, and they sat in silence, the hush between them full of birdsong and rustling leaves.

Emily sighed, letting her eyes wander up and around the garden, tracing the walls of stone that surrounded them. "I used to think I'd be halfway across the world by now. In some desert. Or crawling through a forgotten tomb somewhere."

He glanced over. "You're not?"

"I'm here, remember?" She gestured vaguely. "The closest I get to studying history is cleaning out the stuff modern people leave behind in their modern houses."

He tilted his head. "Why?"

She hesitated. "Because the local job market for archaeologists is actually quite small, believe it or not, and I've still got bills. So, I pick up gigs through the agency where you found me. Usually I help families sort through the giant pile of boxes they found in an attic after someone passes, or their weird hoarder aunt's house packed with antiques. I'll get it ready for an estate sale or for when another family member moves in. Catalog things. Organize what they can't bear to touch."

"That sounds... heavy."

"It can be," she said. "But I like it. I like what people leave behind. What they think matters. It's why I got into archaeology in the first place. I like seeing what's left. Figuring out the story it tells about people after they're gone."

"And the digs?"

She shrugged. "They're hard to get into without funding. Or a position at a university. I've got degrees and passion and a thesis that made my professor cry, but that's not always enough."

He was quiet for a moment. "Still. Seems like the kind of thing someone should fight for."

Emily gave a half-smile. "I am. Just slowly. In the meantime, I have... bills."

The way she hesitated on the last word had Devlin's ears perking up. His brow lifted, and he asked, "And?"

"And what?"

"What else keeps you from pursuing what you love? You say bills, but everyone has bills. If you need a university position, find one here. Or move to somewhere that's hiring. If that's all you need to pursue your dreams..."

"I can't just leave. My life is here."

Devlin's face darkened. "Are you seeing someone? Is that what's keeping you here?"

Emily would've burst out laughing if he hadn't looked so serious, and even then her mouth twitched as she struggled. Shaking her head, she said, "No, nothing like that. Why would I go on a date with you if I'd been seeing someone?"

"You said it wasn't a date," he countered. His face still seemed suspicious, but at least his humor seemed to be returned.

"Touche," she said.

"So?" He didn't mind shamelessly prodding her.

She inhaled deeply, staring at the fingers intertwined with his. He was casually rubbing his thumb along the side of her hand, and she wondered if even realized he was doing it. "I can't leave here because I can't leave my dad."

Devlin's brow lifted. "Your dad?"

"Yes." Her voice flattened. "He's—he needs me."

Devlin didn't press, which made it worse. She didn't want to share any more details, didn't want to even think about it. In fact, she actively spent as little time thinking about it as possible. But here he was, holding her hand and holding space for her without expectation. It surprised her, this tenderness of his. Worse, it made her want to trust him, trust that she could share her secrets with him, and he would keep them (and her) safe.

Her phone buzzed in her pocket. Disentangling her hands from his, she wiggled her phone out of her pocket, glanced at it, and winced. "Speak of the devil."

Without waiting, she stood and walked a few feet away to answer. Her words were stiff, and there were long pauses in between her responses that Devlin couldn't hear.

"Hi, Dad. Yeah, I'm at work. No, I—I can't come now. I know. I know. It'll be okay for now. I'll stop by tomorrow, okay? We'll figure it out then. Don't worry. I'll handle it. I always do."

A pause. She pinched the bridge of her nose with her fingers as if willing more patience into existence.

Then she said more gently, "Just go lie down, okay? Drink some water. I love you."

She ended the call and tucked the phone back into her pocket. She turned back to find Devlin watching her, not with judgment but with something quieter. Something careful.

"I'm sorry," she muttered, rubbing her temple. "He has a way of forgetting that I have a life."

Devlin's voice was calm. "Drugs or alcohol?"

She flinched. Of course he would guess. "Alcohol."

"Was he drunk?"

"Probably. Most days he is."

Still, there was no judgment in his gaze. Emily swallowed, cheeks hot. "I know what you're probably thinking. Poor little working-class girl. Father's an alcoholic, and she's a walking stereotype with daddy issues and an attraction to emotionally unavailable bad boys."

Devlin leaned forward, resting his elbows on his knees. "I wasn't thinking that."

She looked at him with a raised brow and pursed lips, like she didn't believe him for a second.

"Okay, I wasn't thinking all of that," he teased.

She studied him for a moment, and then her patience finally snapped. "I don't know what to make of you. I don't understand you at all. One second you're jumping down my throat, the next you're revealing some deeply held trauma. The last genuine conversation we had was right before you had your hands up my dress, and now you're sitting here *not* being a judgmental asshole about my drunk dad and my daddy issues."

"To be fair, I didn't say you had daddy issues." He gave her a soft smile and patted the bench next to him. "Come back and sit, Em."

Caught off guard and too riled up to argue, she dropped onto the wood next to him with a groan. "Now what?" she asked.

"I wasn't thinking anything bad about you. I was thinking that it must be hard to grow up with a father like that," he said simply. "Yet you still accomplished so much, and you're still standing. That says a lot."

Emily blinked against the sting behind her eyes. "He

wasn't always like this. After my mom died... he just unraveled. I was twelve. It was like watching him die, too, and then suddenly I was the adult. I take care of him, but really I just want my dad back."

Devlin didn't reach for her. Didn't try to fix anything. He just sat there, steady and present.

"I hate that I still feel responsible," she admitted. "That I still clean up after him, check on him, make excuses for him when he doesn't deserve them. I hate that I'm still that little girl hoping that if I try hard enough, he'll get better. If I love him with as little fuss as possible, he'll love me enough to..."

Her voice trailed off, and Devlin saw a tear slide down her cheek. She sniffled, and he was quiet. When her breathing was normal again, he said softly, "You don't have to earn love. No one does. You're enough just as you are."

The words hit her in the chest, and she turned away, pretending to study the tadpoles flitting to and fro in the pond at her feet, blinking fast.

"I rarely talk about this," she murmured.

"I rarely invite people here."

She smiled at that, small and crooked. "Firsts all around."

They sat in the silence that followed, a kind of comfortable-uncomfortable feeling falling over them. Neither was wholly settled with the way it felt to be so vulnerable with someone, but there was some security in that. If nothing else, they were not alone in the feeling. The wind rustled through the vines and leaves and tree branches around them, background noise to their emotions, and a butterfly drifted past, lazy in the late afternoon sun.

When Emily stood to leave, Devlin rose with her. Their eyes met, and for a long moment, neither looked away.

Then, he did something unexpected.

He reached out, not to grab her or pull her closer to him, but just to rest his hand lightly on her cheek, cupping it so delicately it was as if she were made of the finest china. She closed her eyes and inhaled deeply. It had been so long since anyone had touched her in a way that was so intimate and yet not sexual in the least.

Not demanding. Not asking.

Just there.

And somehow, it was exactly what she needed.

11

Two weeks was an awfully long time to think about how the man you were insanely attracted to was a killer. Okay, so maybe he wasn't a killer per se. At least she didn't think he was. Though he had made it very clear that anyone who meddled in his recent business needed to disappear with help. Her assumption of what that meant seemed obvious.

Two weeks since Emily overheard the conversation.

Two weeks of spiraling out about it in her head.

Two weeks since the weight of Devlin's dangerous world had sunk into her bones, reminding her just how deep she was treading.

But during those two weeks, she had kept her head down, and successfully evaded any romantic advances made by Devlin. Her boss, she reminded herself. Not that he had really tried anything, she admitted, but a win was a win.

Burying herself in the work at the manor—letting the hours pass in a blur of dust, books, and family albums—kept her mind busy and her path out of the way of Devlin's, which was just fine with her. The man was a walking contradiction, and she didn't know what to do with him. Or what he wanted with her. Because despite the way he'd all but pounced on her until he actually did, he'd said nothing since.

No acknowledgement of what happened. No further advances. Nothing. Just the constant wondering was enough to drive her to distraction, and she couldn't allow herself to get distracted. Not now, not when there was such a revelation as your potential boyfriend is a killer.

It wasn't every day you came across that conundrum.

Or how much sexier it made him seem. What the fuck was wrong with her?! Not that it was true. She was making a huge assumption based on fragments of a conversation she shouldn't have overheard at all. But if it was true... what the fuck was wrong with her?

Emily couldn't deny the pull toward Devlin—how could she? Every time he entered the room, it was like the temperature went up by ten degrees. She was trying her best to keep herself distant, aloof. The kind of girl his assistant had told her to be, the kind that came and worked and went. Because Devlin was indeed dangerous. He was dark. The man she was slowly falling for was someone she couldn't understand, someone she couldn't fully trust.

Oh god, falling for him? The realization hit her like a

locker door swinging into the face of the awkward nerd in every teen movie ever. She groaned, hating her life more than just a little.

Because not only was she (apparently) falling for him, but she wasn't as upset about what type of man he actually was as she should be. Somewhere between the weeks working here and the night at the restaurant and their afternoon in the garden, something inside her had shifted. Maybe it had shifted for him, too. She wasn't exactly sure, but their connection was growing. That she was sure of.

Today was no different from any other day. She spent hours in the house, this time in a small sitting room off his mother's old room, sorting through old papers and letters half-written or received. Some of them were better suited to the family section of the library, so she walked them to the other wing of the house. She was just finishing when she heard footsteps approaching from down the hall. At first, she thought it was Ms. Voss, Kara, but as the footsteps grew closer, she recognized a different, more familiar sound.

The door to the library creaked open, and she looked up to see Devlin standing there, framed by the doorway. He was as imposing as ever, but there was something different in his demeanor. He was less distant. There was a warmth about him, something more playful. More like he was when his guard was down.

His eyes met hers, and the hardness in them was softer. A small, almost reluctant smile tugged at the corners of his lips.

"Emily," he said, his voice light but still carrying an edge that made it impossible to ignore. "You're still here?"

She blinked, surprised by the shift in tone. Gone was the dangerous, brooding version of Devlin she had come to know. This Devlin—this version of him—felt almost... human. And it unsettled her more than she cared to admit.

"I've got work to do," she replied, trying to sound casual, though her heart fluttered in her chest at the sight of him standing there, his usual aloofness replaced with something almost... playful?

His eyes flicked around the library, taking in the disarray of bookshelves and scattered papers. "It's hard to believe you're actually enjoying this, but I suppose if anyone could find peace in this chaos, it'd be you."

"What is that supposed to mean?"

He shrugged. "Just that you're a tidy soul."

Emily smirked. "It's not so bad. I've got a system. And I like the quiet."

"Is that supposed to be a jab at me for interrupting it?" he asked, stepping into the room fully, closing the door behind him.

Deciding to play along, Emily tucked her tongue in her cheek and shrugged, busying her hands in the stack of books behind her. Technically, none of the books needed sorting, but he didn't know that. She just needed to do something with all this sudden restless energy.

His voice dropped a little, as if sharing a secret. "Or maybe you like this interruption."

Emily's pulse quickened, and she set the book in her

hands down, meeting his gaze. Her breath hitched when Devlin leaned against the wall, trailing a hand over her skin from shoulder to wrist.

"You've been avoiding me," he said.

"I'm not avoiding anyone."

"Are you sure about that?"

She tilted her head slightly, intrigued despite herself. "What do you mean?"

"Every time I've come in here, you're nowhere to be found," he said. He was teasing, but it was with the same underlying intensity that made her heart race. "And when I find you, you look at me like you're deciding whether to run or stay. Then you scamper off like a timid rabbit."

"I'm not timid." Her voice sounded defensive and petulant, and she cringed inwardly.

With his arms crossed over his chest, he watched her with a small smile playing at his lips. "No, you're not."

Emily swallowed, not sure what to say. She didn't like being perceived that way, but now that he said it, she realized he was right. There was a part of her—she hated to admit it—that wanted to run. She probably should. Any sane woman who'd overheard what she had would have run without looking back.

Unfortunately, there was another part, the part she was trying to keep in check, that wanted to stay close to him, to see how far this dangerous attraction would go.

"I don't know what you're talking about." She couldn't think of anything better to say.

Devlin's grin widened. He was clearly enjoying this

exchange far more than she would have liked. "Don't you? Maybe you just don't want to admit that I've gotten under your skin."

Her heart skipped a beat at the way he looked at her. There was something in his gaze—something deep, something that dared her to acknowledge it, to acknowledge him.

"You've got a way of making everything seem... personal. I don't know what you want from me," she said, her voice softer than she intended. The words came out before she could stop them, before she could think better of it.

Devlin adjusted his body, and she could've sworn it moved him closer to her. "Maybe that's because it is personal."

"Oh, really? How?"

He leaned in slightly, lowering his voice to almost a whisper. "I think you know."

Her breath caught in her throat, and her eyes widened. The air sizzled between them, every word and movement electric, as if something was about to explode. Emily's pulse quickened. She could feel the heat radiating off of him, but instead of stepping away, she stood her ground, and she found herself leaning unconsciously toward him.

Suddenly, a sharp knock on the door broke the silence, severing the tension like a thread strung taut and cut. Devlin turned quickly, and Emily gasped and started. She'd nearly forgotten that anyone else in the world existed.

Devlin stepped away from her. "Later," he muttered, his voice still low. "We'll talk more later."

Emily nodded, her entire system reeling from the whiplash. She supposed she should be used to it by now. Though if she was being honest with herself, she wasn't ready for whatever was coming next.

And it was clear now that there was something coming next.

As he left the room, the door clicking softly behind him, Emily stood there, her heart racing. She couldn't decide what she wanted anymore. There was too much information to consider, too many feelings to feel.

With her system raring to go, Emily did the only thing she could think of: she buried herself in work. Even if there were no more work to be done today. Even though the day was nearly over. She couldn't simply go home. That would be admitting defeat.

But no matter how hard she tried to focus, her mind kept drifting back to Devlin. What did he want? What was he doing to her? Why was he so impossible to resist?

Why didn't she want to?

As the minutes eked by, she finally had to admit to herself the futility of her efforts. Admitting defeat or not, she couldn't continue spinning her wheels in here. She was going home, she decided, and she was going to tell the man exactly that.

Did she actually need to? Absolutely not, but she wasn't about to admit that to herself. And so instead of walking straight out that door, she turned down the hallway and let her impulses carry her feet all the way to his study.

She paused outside the door, her hand hovering over the knob. She knew she should keep walking. She should go home, put some space between them and stamp out the embers of desire that burned in her belly. For good. But there was something inside her—something rebellious—that wanted them there, wanting to feel the burn as he fanned them into a blaze.

She turned the handle and stepped inside.

Devlin was sitting at his desk, papers scattered in front of him, the light of his computer screen giving his face a white glow that seemed so out of place in a house like this. His brows were drawn together, and there was a deep line between them, but when he looked up and saw her standing there, his face relaxed. His lips curved into the same small, elusive smile that had been haunting her thoughts every second of the last hour.

"Looking to finish our conversation, Emily?" he teased, the hint of playfulness back in his voice.

Emily shook her head. She wasn't ready to admit she was playing with fire just by being here. "I have nothing to say to you except that I'm finished for the day."

"No?" He stood, coming around the desk slowly and walking toward her. Every movement was purposeful, as if nothing should be wasted. "Then what are you doing here? You don't need to report your comings and goings to me."

"It seemed the polite thing to do." Her pulse raced, but

she wasn't about to back down. "Since we were interrupted earlier."

"Unfortunately."

"Right. Well..." she said, clearing her throat and tapping her fists rhythmically against her thighs. "I'll be going now then. That's all I needed to say."

Devlin's smile grew, and for a moment, the distance between them closed completely. The tension in the room was palpable, his intensity like a pulsing aura surrounding him.

"Good," he said, and suddenly he really was standing mere inches from her. "Because I'm tired of talking."

12

The moment Devlin's lips met hers, all thoughts of restraint, of control, vanished. There was nothing but raw hunger, the kind that twisted his gut, burned in his veins. His hands gripped her fiercely, pulling her against him as though he couldn't get close enough. His kiss was demanding, urgent, each movement guided by a primal need that wasn't meant to be denied.

Emily moaned into his mouth as he deepened the kiss, his tongue sweeping past her lips, claiming her with a hunger that made her pulse quicken. She hadn't expected it to be like this—hadn't expected the way their fire consumed everything in its path. There was no room for hesitation now. She melted against him, giving in to the heat, to the overwhelming pull of him.

She was utterly and completely under his spell.

Devlin's hands moved quickly, urgently, his hands shoving away her clothing as though he was starving for the feel of her skin beneath his. Emily moaned again as his hands traced the lines of her body, his touch possessive. The electricity had been building between them for weeks.

His lips left hers only to move down her neck, trailing soft kisses that turned quickly into bites, each one more desperate than the last. She felt them dig deep into her flesh, and she revelled in the way he was marking her as his. Only his.

Her breaths turned into pants, and her hands pulled at his shirt, tearing the hem tucked into his pants and ripping at buttons. She needed him, needed the roughness of his touch, the feel of him buried deep inside her. There was no room for gentleness. He wasn't asking. He was taking.

Devlin ground his hips into her, and his hands made quick work of her pants, and Emily responded to him in kind, her body moving instinctively against his, her hands grabbing the edges of her shirt and trying to pull it over her head. But Devlin was in control.

He lifted his head away from her neck long enough to say, "No."

Then his mouth was on hers again, and he was lifting her, his hands under her ass. She wrapped her legs around him instinctively, the motion pushing his hard cock against her pussy. He walked her to his desk, setting her down without a care about what she sat on. He ground against her, groaning as the movement teased them both.

The world outside the office ceased to exist. There was nothing but him. Nothing but the way he kissed her, touched her, his body pressing against hers with a need so strong it was almost suffocating.

His hands were everywhere now, and he finally drew her shirt from her body, letting the fabric flutter to the floor. Her bra quickly followed, and then his mouth was on her breasts, pressing her nipple in hard circles with the flat of his tongue, suckling it, taking the tip between his teeth. She gasped, and he pulled away from her with a grin.

"Do you like what I do to you, love?"

Emily's legs shook, and she nodded yes over and over again.

"Do you want me to tell you what else I want to do to you?"

She nodded again, but he shook his head. "No, no, no. You're going to have to do better than that. Tell me how much you want to hear it. Tell me you want me to take it," he ordered.

"Fuck, Devlin. Tell me what you're going to do to me. Take it. I want you to take all of it," she begged.

"Mmmmm, that's a good girl," he said, drawing back so he could unbutton his shirt one button at a time, watching her hungrily as she panted and writhed under his gaze. "You want me to fuck you right here on my desk? Stretch that pretty little pussy out with this cock? I'll bet it's dripping for me already. I'll have to taste it first, take that clit in my mouth, fill you up with my fingers until you squirt all in my mouth."

Her eyes widened, and so did his smile. "Has anyone made you do that before?"

"No," she said, her voice breathy and far away.

"Perfect," he said. His pants undone, they hung from his hips, leaving his cock hard and throbbing between them. He pushed aside her underwear. His fingers circled her clit until her eyes glazed over, until her legs shook and she pushed against him. "Because it's mine. You're mine. Every orgasm, every moan of pleasure, is mine from now until forever. Every time you cum, you'll think of me."

He knew she was close; he could hear it in her moans, see it in the way she moved. He kept the pace of his fingers steady, his mouth to her ear, encouraging her every step of the way with hot whispers in her ear.

When she cried out, and her back arched, he smiled against her skin. Then he dove his fingers into her pussy, the wet walls pulsing around him. He curved his fingers until he found that one special spot tucked up behind her pelvic bone. Kneeling before her, he took her clit in his mouth and sucked hard again and again, his fingers fucking her hard and fast.

"Fuck! Oh my god—no—" she screamed, pushing at his head and trying to wiggle away from him, her body far too sensitive for this much sensation.

But his arm snaked around her waist and held her in place. He lifted his mouth far enough from her clit that he could talk, his fingers still slamming into her, building her body back up for something she couldn't quite name. "Cum for me," he demanded.

Then it was as if the floodgates opened, and a strange sensation flooded her body with warmth. A slick, slippery fluid poured out of her, and Devlin groaned with pleasure as it soaked her underwear, the desk, and everything she'd been sitting on. But he didn't stop moving. Before she could even process what was happening, his mouth was back on her clit. She cried out as he forced another orgasm from her, and she collapsed backward on the desk, scattering papers and pens and god knows what else.

"Do you like how I take care of my pussy?" he asked, positioning the tip of his cock inside the outer folds of her.

"Oh, yes," she moaned, every part of her body like tingly jello.

"Tell me whose pussy that is," he said, pushing inside her millimeter by millimeter.

"It's your pussy," she panted.

"That's right. Because you're mine." He sank inside her, and the world spun. She felt herself unraveling under him. He slid out of her and then thrust deep inside, pushing even farther this time. He demanded, "Tell me!"

"Yours," she breathed. "I'm yours."

"Mine," he growled, pumping into her wet heat with a kind of dark urgency, each thrust deep and possessive, pulling moans from her lips as if he could reach deep inside her and touch every hidden part of her.

The heat of the moment built, their bodies moving together as if they were made for this, for each other. When neither could go any higher, when they couldn't bear to stave off the climax any longer, it was like an explosion.

Emily's back arched, her nails digging into his skin, her

body shaking as Devlin's name slipped from her lips in a breathless gasp. He didn't slow his rhythm. He followed her, his own release coming with a rough, low growl as he buried his face in her neck, his body tensing, holding onto her as if he were anchoring himself to something real.

When it was over, the silence was deafening. Emily's heart hammered in her chest as she tried to catch her breath. She wanted to wonder what would happen now. It would be on brand for her brain to kick into overdrive, to race with a hundred thoughts at once, but she felt so deliciously used and sated that she couldn't bear to ruin it for herself.

Before she could spend too much time doing any thinking, though, Devlin was moving. He didn't speak, merely lifted her off the desk as if she weighed nothing. She didn't even have time to process what was happening. One moment, she lay on his desk enjoying the ripples of her many orgasms and the raw, throbbing feeling between her legs. The next, she was being carried through the halls of Moore Manor. She didn't protest. She couldn't.

When they reached his bedroom, Devlin placed her gently on the bed, his movements surprisingly tender now that the storm had passed. But his expression was unreadable. He remained silent. When she was settled, he slid into bed beside her, pulling her close as though it was the most natural thing in the world.

For a long moment, there was nothing but silence between them. Emily lay there, her head on his chest, her body still tingling. She could hear his heart beating, steady and calm beneath her ear, and for the first time, the weight of the evening settled over her. Devlin's fingers tightened in her hair, and the arm around her shoulders held her just a little more securely. She wasn't sure what to make of this, but as sleep quickly claimed her, she found she wasn't ready to care.

Tomorrow was soon enough for the real world to come and burst her bubble.

It always did.

13

he bells over the door tinkled as Devlin stepped inside Sips Cafe and Coffeehouse, a modest coffee shop by the looks of it and one that seemed to try too hard to feel like home. Among the chalkboard menus, homemade muffins, and effortlessly mismatched chairs, there was a frantic energy.

It smelled of cinnamon and espresso and desperation.

Devlin wrinkled his nose and attempted to relax his body, drawing a slow breath in and allowing his eyes to scan the room. From head to toe, every movement was purposeful. This wasn't exactly the ideal place for this type of meeting in his opinion, but Emily's father had chosen the place.

He spotted the man easily. Liam Hartwell sat near the back window, nursing a lukewarm cup of coffee like it owed him something. He wore a wrinkled button-up, his hair combed but overly flat and slick with too much oil, as if he rarely styled it so neatly.

Devlin got the impression that he was trying to appear put together, trying not to show how far he'd fallen. Good. At least he had some semblance of shame, he thought to himself.

He crossed the room, and his voice was brisk when he spoke. "Mr. Hartwell."

Devlin arranged himself artfully in one of the cracked leather chairs across from the man. He didn't offer a handshake, choosing to brush a hand down the front of his shirt instead. Liam looked up, startled at first. He squinted as if trying to place him, as if they hadn't actually had an entire conversation to set up this meeting in the first place.

"You're... Emily's employer?" he asked.

"Devlin Moore."

"Right. Of course. Mr. Moore." Liam chuckled nervously and picked up his coffee mug with shaking hands. "Didn't expect to meet under such formal terms. Emily didn't mention—"

"She doesn't know."

Liam paused, the coffee halfway to his mouth. "She doesn't know what?"

Devlin leaned forward, elbows resting on his knees, and clasped his hands together. Liam sank back into the chair, his expression of confusion turning to nervousness. "That I asked to meet you."

"But why?" Liam asked. "Is Emily in some kind of trouble?"

Devlin cocked his head, his eyes taking on an intensity that was equally possessive and angry. "Is she?" he countered, raising his brow pointedly.

"I don't know what you mean." Liam shifted in his seat uncomfortably.

Devlin couldn't tell if he was guilty, confused, or drunk, but he had little patience for the man. If it weren't for this pull to protect Emily, to give her everything he could, he wouldn't be wasting his time here at all. He wasn't ready to question the feeling or try to understand it, but he needed to do something about it.

"I think you do. I think you know exactly what your daughter gives up to care for you, what she has sacrificed her entire life to do."

"I don't know what you're talking about."

"Oh? You don't call her in the middle of the night? Steal her debit card and hit the ATM? Text her begging for food because you spent the money for it on cheap booze?" Devlin's voice was calm, clear, matter-of-fact. He sat unbothered, looking at Emily's father as if he were a bug smashed across his windshield: disgusting and inconvenient.

"How do you know about that?" Liam's eyes widened, and he wiped a bead of sweat from his forehead.

"That isn't your concern, but it ends now."

"Now, you listen here!" Liam sputtered. "You can't just barge in and meddle with things you don't know nothin' about. I don't know who you—"

Devlin held up a hand, and despite his outrage, Liam

seemed to know enough to silence himself immediately. "I'm offering you an eighteen-month sobriety program. Inpatient to start. You'll live there for a year with access to physical, medical, and psychological care. The best money can buy. Then you'll move into a transition program where you'll live independently with support for the duration of the program."

"You're... not going to tell Emily? About the..." Liam stuttered. "The things she doesn't know."

"That you lie and steal from her? She's a smart woman. She knows," Devlin countered.

Liam considered that. He brought the mug to his mouth finally and took two deep gulps of the hot liquid. "Why would you—" Liam started, blinking rapidly. "You're serious?"

"I don't joke about things like this."

"I don't need a program."

"No," Devlin said. "You don't. Emily does. Every time she covers your mess, rearranges her life to care for you, picks up the phone at all hours to talk you down—she is kinder to you than you deserve. You don't need a program, but if you love her, you should want one."

Liam stiffened, wounded. "I love my daughter."

"Then prove it," Devlin said evenly. "Get help. Not later. Now."

Silence stretched between them. Liam looked down at the mug in his hands. His face shifted between guilt and shame and stubbornness, the face of a man who'd failed his daughter and didn't know how to face it. "I've tried. Before. You know? Rehab. Cold turkey. It doesn't... stick."

"That sounds like a conversation to have with your doctor when you check in," Devlin said. "A car is already waiting outside to take you."

He gulped, and his eyes widened and jerked toward the glass windows at the front of the coffee shop. "Now?" His hands shook.

Devlin nodded, his face a mask of stone, his eyes hardened to match. "Emily deserves a life that isn't built around saving you."

Liam's eyes filled, and he blinked rapidly. "She's all I've got."

"Act like it." His voice was flat. Devlin slid a folder across the table. Inside were intake forms, travel arrangements, a schedule, insurance paperwork for a policy he didn't have yesterday. Everything he needed for his stay. "It's time to go."

Devlin stood, and Liam looked dazed. "I don't even— how am I supposed to—?"

"There's nothing to figure out."

Liam's throat worked. "What happens if I say no?"

Devlin's voice was quiet, deadly calm, like the silence that descends upon a forest when all the animals sense a predator is among them. "You won't."

There was no threat in it, not directly, but the finality in Devlin's tone and the way he grabbed Liam's upper arm to lead him toward the door left no room for debate. This was not a negotiation or an intervention. This was an order.

Liam sagged, deflated, and allowed himself to be led to the waiting car out front. The driver opened the back door. Before getting in, he turned back and met Devlin's emotionless gaze. "She deserves better."

"She does."

Devlin slammed the car door, heedless of the impact of his words. Managing that was now the job of the countless and incredibly highly paid therapists at the rehabilitation center. He nodded to the driver and watched the car pull away from the curb.

He kept watching long after it disappeared into traffic, though he wasn't sure why.

14

When Devlin returned to the manor, the house was warm with late morning light. The sun poured through the tall windows in golden ribbons, catching the dust motes and softening the edges of the grand old place.

He found Emily in the vast expanse of his family's library. She was perched on a stool he'd noticed she favored near the west wall. She was sitting in front of a stack of what looked like portfolios next to what was clearly art made by children. Her hair was pinned up, and an old pencil was tucked behind her ear. She looked like chaos and competence and temptation all wrapped into one.

"I thought I'd find you here," he said.

Her head jerked up in surprise, brow furrowed and eyes wary. Then the wash of confusion disappeared from her face, and she smiled indulgently. "I'm always here."

"What are you doing?" he asked, his brows drawing together as he recognized the childhood drawings.

Emily looked up at him with a smile stretched across her face and virtually glowed. She kicked her feet happily, and he wondered if she knew it was a habit of hers when she was pleased with something.

"I'm organizing your school art. Yours and Sophia's. Your mother—er, I guess it could've been your father—may have tossed them into a big box, but she was pretty consistent about writing the name and date on them. I decided to put them into an album," she said.

Devlin looked down at her work so far, taking hold of a few of the pages and flipping them back and forth. Almost absentmindedly, he said, "Speaking of fathers, yours is going to rehab," he said.

Hands that had been so busy with the task at hand froze. "What?" she sputtered.

"He's checking into an eighteen month program tomorrow. It will start with intensive inpatient care and transition to independent living support eventually. It's all been arranged. He's on his way there now."

Emily blinked, and her mouth gaped. She shook her head in disbelief. "I—I'm sorry, how do you even know who my father is?"

"I make it a point to know the things that matter."

"That's not an answer." She folded her arms, a hint of frustration giving her voice an edge.

Devlin folded his arms in return, mirroring her. "You mentioned him. That was enough."

She narrowed her eyes. She couldn't figure out whether he was playing with her or mocking her. "You found him? Arranged this? Without telling me?"

"Yes."

"And he agreed to go?"

"I didn't give him much choice."

Emily blinked, stunned into silence, and her arms dropped to her sides. She wasn't sure how to feel about it, nevermind what to say. Relief warred with worry as her thoughts raced.

"How much will it cost?" Her voice was quieter. The reality of what this would mean for her was setting in—the reality of the challenges of a life Devlin knew nothing about.

Her father didn't have health insurance, though she knew she could apply for state insurance on his behalf. She doubted he wouldn't qualify. Though she worried if a facility chosen by the sickeningly wealthy Devlin Moore would even take state-funded insurance. She'd looked into it once or twice before, and the number of facilities that were self-pay only was depressing. This would likely be the same. It was almost certain, and there was no way she could pay for it. Which meant that even if her father made it to the program, she couldn't afford to keep him there.

"It doesn't matter."

"It matters a great deal to me," she said, coming to her feet so quickly that she nearly upended her stool. A flush of temper stained the lower half of her cheeks splotchy pink. "You may not have to live life under the iron thumb of a budget, but some of us do. You don't get to just make decisions that affect people's finances without talking to them."

"Did I say anything about money?"

Stunned, she replied, "No."

"No, I didn't."

"I don't understand." The words spilled out of her mouth as slow as molasses, as if every syllable was being pulled out like gum from the bottom of a shoe.

He shrugged. "It's paid for. Consider it part of your benefits package."

She laughed once—sharp, startled. "I don't get benefits."

"You do now."

She stared at him, lips parted. "You're serious." Emily sat down again slowly, her legs like rubber beneath her. "Why?"

He tilted his head. "Do you want the bitter truth or the sentimental one?"

"Both."

"The bitter truth?" He stepped closer, his voice even. "Because your father is a liability to your life, your career, your peace of mind. You won't move forward as long as you're chained to him."

Emily nodded slowly and chewed the inside of her cheek. "And the sentimental one?"

Devlin's eyes bore into hers with an intensity that left her breathless. "Because you're mine."

"I'm not."

"Yes. You are."

Emily closed her eyes, pinching the bridge of her nose and inhaling so deeply that her nostrils flared. His assistant's warning echoed in her mind, and still she'd allowed it to get this far. She'd walked right into his shadow, and how she was struggling to keep her flame lit.

"We'll argue about that another day then." Focusing on the issue at hand and not how dangerous it was to be the object of this man's possessiveness, she looked down at her lap. "I don't know what to say except thank you. For my father."

"I didn't do it for him."

He took a step closer to her, and the knot in her stomach tightened. Whether it was desire or fear, she wasn't sure, but she suspected it was far worse. Perhaps it was both.

"No, you didn't," she said simply, her shoulders lifting in the smallest of shrugs.

The silence between them felt suddenly as taut as a wire pulled between heartbeats, like the tightly wound string of an instrument, and every choice they made was a finger plucking at the string. In a perfect world, she'd imagine that would make the most beautiful music. Here, she wasn't so sure what sound it would make.

"I'm not staying forever, Devlin," she said finally. Her voice was barely a whisper carried along the dusty air currents of the library.

He nodded once, jaw tight. "I know."

"Do you?"

"No." The word was a growl. Honest and raw.

Emily cocked her head and raised a brow, crossing her arms in challenge. "Are you proposing I stay and continue dusting the shelves of your private family museum forever, then?"

Devlin stared at her. As the sunlight brushed over her skin, at the anger and confusion in her expression. At the subtle shimmer in her eyes that betrayed her, that all but shouted that maybe—just maybe—she didn't want to leave as much as she claimed.

"I don't know," he said.

With a sigh, she stepped past him, her fingers itching to trail across his shoulders or back as she walked by. She resisted the impulse, and when she thought back on that moment later, she wouldn't know whether she regretted that.

She paused at the door, looking back at him over her shoulder. "I'm going home early today. I think you'll understand." Then she left, her departure so quiet he didn't hear her footsteps echo down the hallway nor the opening or closing of the front door.

He didn't say goodbye. He didn't say anything.

Instead, he watched her go, ears straining to catch the sounds of her leaving. For longer than would ever admit, he remained a statue there in the dimly lit room. Already he missed her presence, and he wondered how the hell he'd survive the day she walked out for good.

15

The phone call was exactly as much of a headache as Devlin feared.

His ex-business partners—men he had once trusted, even if he found them young and impulsive—were growing impatient. They didn't like being refused. They didn't like being told no. And now, they were threatening him, demanding that he proceed with the next shipment as if working together was still an option.

A shipment he had refused, an arms deal he no longer wanted to be a part of. The people he had thought he could control had become the very thing that threatened to unravel everything.

Devlin leaned back in his chair, the phone pressed tightly to his ear as the voice on the other end became colder, more insistent.

"You'll go through with the deal, Moore," the voice purred, the tone too smooth, too confident. "We've made our demands clear, and if you don't comply, we'll make sure you regret it."

Regret it? Even their threat sounded childish. Devlin took a deep breath, considering how best to respond. On one hand, he wanted nothing more to do with the twins. As far as he was concerned, their partnership was over. On the other hand, he didn't want to escalate them either. There was no point in risking it, however hollow their threats. He rubbed circles on his temples where a headache was building.

"The deal is off, as are all future contracts. My decision is final," Devlin said.

There was silence, and he thought perhaps the call was over. The twins would curse and moan, maybe even drum up a modicum of trouble. Then, this would blow over. They should wrap it up in a matter of days, a couple of weeks max.

"We know who you're protecting," the voice said.

Devlin's chest tightened as the words hit him like a punch to the gut.

The voice continued, a sickening smugness threading through the words. "We'll make sure she's taken care of if you don't follow through. You really think you can walk away from this? You know better than anyone else that it doesn't work like that."

This wasn't business anymore. This was a warning. But he couldn't back down, not if he wanted them to push the line back every time.

"We are done," Devlin bit out, his voice hard, but a

storm was brewing beneath his calm facade. "I won't change my mind, and you can't threaten me into submission. I have nothing left to lose."

The voice on the other end let out a low chuckle, one that sent a chill down Devlin's spine. "Oh, it's not a threat, Moore. It's a guarantee. Fulfill the contract, or we make sure she pays the price for your mistake."

Devlin's pulse quickened as the full weight of the threat sank in. They knew about Emily. They were using her to force his hand. His mind raced as he gripped the desk, his knuckles white. He wanted to believe the twins were all talk, inept children who never would've succeeded in this industry if it hadn't been handed to them on a silver platter. The truth was, what they lacked in sense they made up for in brutality. If they knew about Emily, the only thing that mattered now was keeping her safe.

The picture of his sister drew his gaze, her smiling face looking back at him just as it always did. The stab of grief was instant, a sharp ripping feeling that tore right through his chest. He couldn't go through that again. He couldn't fail someone he cared about again.

"The choice is yours."

Devlin's jaw tightened. He hadn't known it would come to this, but hearing it out loud made his blood run cold. Emily was caught in the crossfire of his world—a world she never should have been a part of. His world, his mistakes.

"Touch her, and you'll regret it," Devlin growled, his

voice taking on an edge that was sharp enough to cut through steel.

The voice chuckled again, a hollow, mirthless laugh. "We'll see how long your resolve lasts. You've already lost more than you think. We'll be watching. And when you fail... we'll make sure she's the one who suffers."

The line went dead, leaving nothing but a ringing silence in its wake. Devlin dropped the phone onto the desk, the weight of the threat hanging heavily over him. They knew about Emily. They knew how far he would go to protect something of his. And now, they were going to use her against him.

He stood, pacing the length of the room. His mind was a storm of rage and fear, his thoughts scattered as the realization hit him. This wasn't about business or a family legacy or his pride. It was about survival. His. Hers.

He couldn't lose her. He wouldn't.

Devlin's hands clenched into fists, the anger inside him bubbling to the surface, but he had to keep it together. He had to think. He picked up the phone and dialed Kara, his fingers pressing the keys with more force than necessary. She picked up after the second ring.

"Mr. Moore. How can I help you?"

"Kara," he said, his voice controlled but tight. "I want a private security detail on Emily Hartwell. Immediately."

There was a long pause on the other end before Kara spoke, her voice measured. "What's going on, Devlin? What happened?"

Devlin's voice hardened as he spoke, the words coming

out clipped, impatient. "Just do it. I need a team in place for her. And I don't want her to know about it. Keep this quiet."

Kara's voice dropped, a hint of disbelief creeping in. "You can't be serious. If it's the twins retaliating—"

"I'm not asking for your opinion, Kara," Devlin snapped, cutting her off. His patience was running thin. His chest heaved as the weight of the situation settled in. "Do what I say. I'll handle the rest. Just make sure Emily stays safe. Do you understand?"

There was a tense silence before Kara responded. "Understood. But this will not end well."

Devlin clenched his jaw, not wanting to hear her doubts. "I'll deal with it," he said coldly, hanging up before she could respond.

He stood there for a moment, his hands shaking at his sides. Devlin couldn't let them get to her, had to keep her safe, whatever the cost. He couldn't back down. Not now. Not when Emily was on the line.

Devlin turned toward the window, his gaze sweeping over the vast grounds. His eyes fell on Emily walking through the garden, her silhouette framed by the fading light of the day. She was so far removed from all of this. She shouldn't be involved. She should have been kept far away from the chaos of his world.

But there she was, moving through the grounds with that quiet grace, unaware of the danger lurking just beneath the surface.

Devlin's gaze hardened as he watched her, his resolve

solidifying. He couldn't afford to keep her close. Not now. Not if it meant putting her at risk. He couldn't let this touch her, even if that meant he needed to stay away from her. But the more he convinced himself that it was the correct option, the only option, the more the thought of it felt impossible. How could he stay away now? How could he pull away from what he had so thoroughly claimed?

But he had to. He couldn't drag her into the mess he had created.

And so, as Emily continued her walk, oblivious to the storm brewing around her, Devlin made a vow to himself. He would stay away from her. For her safety. For his own sanity.

He would protect her, even if it meant sacrificing his heart to do it.

16

The days that followed were heavy with silence as Emily battled confusion, anger, and hurt in equal measure. Devlin was pulling away from her, retreating into a coldness she didn't know how to thaw. It was like the man she knew, the man she had cared for, had disappeared entirely, retreated into a castle with thick stone walls and raised the drawbridge. In his place was someone unrecognizable.

He avoided her, kept his distance, his eyes filled with an unreadable hardness. And when he spoke to her, his words were brief, curt, almost dismissive.

It hurt more than Emily would admit. But she wasn't ready to give up on him. Yet.

She couldn't. Not when everything between them felt like it was beginning to be more.

But Devlin wouldn't let her in. No matter how hard she

tried, no matter how many times she tried to ask him why he was shutting her out, he wouldn't answer. His eyes would simply go cold, as if the blinds were coming down on them, and he would turn and walk away. The walls between them grew higher every day. And she could feel it. She could feel him pulling away, slipping further from her reach with every passing minute.

Each day Emily felt a bit more helpless, like she was drowning in a sea of confusion and longing. She watched him from a distance as he moved through the house, his jaw tight, his eyes constantly scanning for something she couldn't see. He was locked in his head, consumed by something she couldn't touch.

She didn't understand what had caused him to pull away. Had she done something, said something wrong? After everything that had happened, the distance between them was unbearable. The emptiness in her chest, the absence of the connection they'd shared so briefly, was more than she could stand.

After days of waiting, wondering, hurting, she had to know. She couldn't stomach this feeling or the pitiful look she knew was in her eyes when they crossed paths. She deserved an explanation at the very least. She wasn't a toy to be pulled off the shelf and played with on a whim.

Filled with righteous indignation, Emily set her resolve and marched toward the study, hoping to find Devlin, hoping to catch him when he wasn't avoiding her. He wasn't there. She checked the parlor, a few random (and pointless in her opinion) sitting rooms, and the kitchen. Out of breath and now worked up to a proper mad, she finally found him in his office, his back to her, standing at the window with his hand resting against the glass. His posture was rigid; his face impassive.

"Devlin," she said, her voice sharper than she'd intended. "We need to talk."

He didn't turn, didn't even acknowledge her presence at first. His silence was like a slap, but she would not back down now.

"Devlin," she repeated, the anger pouring over the word like a wash of red paint. With her mouth set in a thin line, she crossed her arms over her chest.

He turned, his expression unreadable, his eyes cold. "There's nothing to talk about, Emily."

Her heart sank at the finality in his tone, and it was sheer temper that kept her from dissolving into a puddle of tears and fleeing. She stepped closer, her arms dropping to her side, brows pulling together and eyes searching his face for any trace of the man who had been so warm, so tender with her.

"Why are you doing this?" she asked, her voice barely above a whisper.

He didn't respond immediately. The silence between them stretched out, and she could feel the walls thick between them as if they were literally in the room. It was as if he were closing himself off from her completely.

"You're pushing me away," she continued, her voice

trembling with frustration. "I don't understand. What happened? What did I do?"

Devlin's eyes narrowed, and for the first time, she saw the faintest flicker of pain behind the coldness, but it was gone as quickly as it came, replaced by a sharp, almost angry edge.

"I'm protecting you," he said, his voice low and tight. "From myself."

"Do I look like a woman in need of protection? What kind of archaic patriarchal bullshit is that?" she demanded.

"You wouldn't understand."

"Oh, so cryptic and sexist. Wonderful." Her voice was flat, dripping with the sarcasm she wore like a cloak. She'd be damned if she would show him her pain now. Not here. Not like this.

He rubbed a finger over his eye, almost as if the conversation was an annoyance. He sighed and turned his body toward her. "You don't belong in my world. You don't belong in my world."

Emily shook her head, her chest aching. "What does that even mean, Devlin? You think you're protecting me by shutting me out? Pushing me away? That's not protecting me, that's—"

"Enough," he interrupted, his voice cold and firm. "I've made my decision."

"Your decision?" Emily repeated, her voice rising. "What decision, Devlin? To make sure I stay in the dark?

To make sure I'm kept at arm's length while you drown in whatever this is? I don't want that. I want you. But you're too busy pushing me away to see that."

Devlin's jaw clenched, and for a moment, the room felt like it was closing in on them. He took a step forward, his eyes locked on hers. His voice was clipped, distant. "You were a mistake."

She reared back in pain, and then her temper flared to new heights. She closed the distance between them and met his fiery gaze with her own. Drawing back her arm, she slapped him hard across the cheek.

Devlin's expression darkened, and before she could react, the back of his hand connected with her cheek, throwing her to the floor. She cried out, her eyes wide and instantly filled with hot tears. She raised a hand to touch her face where the reddened skin burned hot, and he leaned down, a hand snaking out and grabbing her wrist.

"Get out and don't come back."

Emily yanked her wrist from his grip, rubbing the smarting skin where he'd held it like a vice. "Don't ever fucking touch me again," Emily said, her voice shaking with emotion.

She did her best to pull her body up with some dignity and walked out of the room, her heart pounding in her chest and head held high. She no longer cared about finding answers or finishing some story that had nothing to do with her or her family. Not now. Not after everything this. He was ready to throw it all away, to hurt her, mentally and physically. Fine.

She deserved better than to be yanked around, treated like a disposable plaything, and then assaulted when she demanded better. Fuck him, she thought, her hand dashing away the hot tears that spilled down her cheeks.

She made her way to the library, where she'd left her bag, before she finally collapsed. Dropping into a chair, she let the sobs wash over her like an ocean wave pulling her under. The feel of this room, the sight and smell of it, ripped away her remaining defenses and left her open and raw.

Was she really so worthless to him that the conquest was all he cared about? That he could care so little for her, that he could treat her with so little regard? Hurt her so deeply? She'd thought they were building something, connecting, but it was a farce. She was just another pastime for the wealthy and bored.

Now that he was done with her, she was no longer needed.

She didn't want to believe that was true. She wanted to believe he desired her, and more than that, that he cared for her. But she couldn't delude herself into thinking that anymore. She'd been wrong, so deeply wrong. She'd played with fire, and now the pain from the burns was her only company.

Taking a deep breath, she tried to pull back the emotions raging inside her. She refused to be consumed by them, but try as she might, she couldn't stop the flow of tears. So she stopped trying. She threw her bag over her shoulder and stood, doing her best to navigate the room, bleary eyes and all.

Damn her tears. Damn Devlin Moore. Damn this job. Damn this entire place.

She was going home.

Her feet led her down the hallway, largely by muscle memory as she desperately blinked away the moisture in her eyes and sniffled. Suddenly, things began to look different, darker. She realized she must have taken a wrong turn in this maze of a house. She just wanted to go home, cry in peace, and possibly drink the biggest glass of wine of her life.

Emily looked around and groaned out loud. She was sure she hadn't been in this part of the house before. So lost in her own thoughts and blinded by her tears, she hadn't been paying attention to where she was going, and now she had no idea how to get back to where she'd been.

She paused, her shoes scuffing the worn wooden floor beneath them. She recognized nothing. It was darker here, the air thickened with dust and the heavy smell of mold, like it had been untouched for years. Finally able to see, Emily sniffled again and began looking for any clue that might help her find her way back to the main hall.

Turning in circles, her eyes darted up and down the hallway. She started in one direction and made a few turns before backtracking and trying again. Twice. What idiot designed this godforsaken floor plan? And why was it necessary to have so many rooms in one house? How could anyone ever need or use this much space? She wondered and wandered, her hand unconsciously rubbing the soreness of her face.

Stopping to get her bearings again, she noticed a door in front of her. It was slightly ajar, and something about it pulled at her. She couldn't quite explain it, but she would one day look back on this moment and say it was like the house wanted her to find it. Almost without thinking, she pushed the door open.

And froze in place when she saw the room inside.

It appeared to be a sort of private study. A room no one had ever mentioned before, tucked away in a secluded part of the house. It was cold and dim, filled with old furniture and bookshelves stacked with more dusty books. There was something strangely intimate about it—the way personal effects were scattered about the room, a hairbrush of tarnished silver, a hand mirror with the gold gilding partially rubbed off, a single evening glove of dark silk. They were things that had belonged to people who had lived here long before, evidence of the daily machinations of life.

Emily's heart thudded in her chest as she stepped deeper into the room, her eyes taking in the surrounding items. Letters, pictures, and dried roses littered the tables and shelves. Some roses were bent and broken, their petals brittle and dry, while others still lay across tables, their stems twisted and lifeless.

She picked up a small card, thick with dust, and blew it off. Her fingers trembled as she turned it over and saw the name: Sophia Moore.

Devlin's sister.

It was a funeral announcement, and the finality of it hit her like a blow to the chest. She looked around the room with fresh eyes, noticing now the portraits of a man and two women, people she knew were Devlin's father, mother, and sister. This room wasn't just an abandoned part of the house. It was a manifestation of loss, a room transformed into a capsule for grief, for Devlin's grief. And, judging by how poorly it was cared for, his shame and guilt over their deaths.

She was reaching for a family photo, torn so that only a tiny hand—she assumed it was Devlin's—remained alongside his mother, father, and sister, when the door slammed open. Devlin stood before her, his face twisted in fury.

"What the hell are you doing here?" he snapped.

Emily's breath caught in her throat, and she stumbled back, the photo fluttering to the floor at her feet. "I—I got lost... I didn't mean to—" she stuttered, but Devlin's anger was a tidal wave that swept over her.

"Get out!" he growled, the sound low and vicious. He shoved past her, his fists clenched as he knocked over a table, sending it and everything on it crashing to the floor.The sound was deafening.

Emily's heart raced as Devlin's fury consumed him. He grabbed a vase, his movements swift and violent, and smashed it against the wall, sending shards of glass flying across the room. The sight of him so consumed by rage terrified her, but her body refused to move.

"Get out!" he bellowed, this time his voice a mixture of pain and rage at full volume.

Her eyes widened, her pulse raced, and at least her feet came unglued. She turned and fled from the room, moving as fast as her legs would carry her. She ran blindly until she somehow stumbled out a side door and into the open air, and she kept running until she was safely in her car.

She didn't look back, not even once.

Emily's hands trembled as she stepped out of her car, the key to her apartment building slipping between her fingers. The tears wouldn't stop. They'd come in waves, hitting her all at once, receding long enough for her to catch her breath, then battering her anew until she was drowning again. Her last moments with Devlin kept replaying in her head, a symphony of temper and aggression and confusion.

Her vision blurred as she fumbled with the key, struggling to get it into the lock. The wooden door, flanked by stone columns and masonry, loomed over her as if judging her as weak as she felt. She was exhausted, emotionally and physically drained from weeks that felt like years. The weight of it sat heavily on her chest. She wanted to go inside, close the door, and forget about all of it. Pretend none of it had ever happened.

"Please just fucking work," she begged as her shaking

hands refused to cooperate and the key yet again slipped from the knob.

She didn't hear the footsteps behind her, didn't have any time to react or even scream. It wasn't until a man grabbed her from behind that she realized she wasn't alone outside and hadn't been for some time. A rough hand clamped over her mouth, an arm snaking around her torso and pulling her backward. The cold, sharp blade of a knife dug into her throat. She tried to gasp, but the seal over her mouth was too tight. Her nostrils flared, and her body stiffened in shock and pain as the blade bit into her skin. Her heart raced as panic set in.

She tried to scream, tried to break free, but it did nothing but cause the knife to dig deeper into her skin. Her eyes, wide and wild, looked around for anything, anyone, that could help. The man's grip on her tightened, even as she kicked and struggled.

A voice from behind her, low and menacing, whispered in her ear, "Quiet or I'll cut your throat and gut you from tit to cunt."

She made a small noise of pain as he pressed the knife in to drive his point home, but she stopped fighting, heart thundering in her chest as a dark realization settled in: she was helpless and alone.

A second man joined the first, zip tying her wrists behind her back and grabbing the legs that dragged across the paved walkway before her stumbling could slow them down. She tried to get her bearings, tried to make sense of what was happening, but her mind was spinning. All she could hear was the sound of her own breath, rasping and ragged, but she had to push through the panic and the fear.

It took every ounce of her strength to shove it down and focus. If her true crime addiction had taught her anything, it was that every detail mattered. She looked around as they shoved her into a van, straining her eyes and committing everything she could to memory. The first man skirted the hood and climbed into the driver's seat while the second man crawled in after her, sliding the door closed behind him as they pulled away as silently as they'd arrived.

The man next to her noticed her sharp gaze scanning her surroundings and caught her chin between her fingers. He yanked her face toward him, his eyes boring into hers from behind his black mask. "Stop that."

He reached down and pulled a dark cloth from the floor. Emily struggled against it as he wrapped it around her eyes and wound up with her head violently shoved against the metal shell of the car. Stars danced in her vision as the force of the blow stunned her, but there was no time to register the pain. Before she could even recover, the man stomped on her stomach, knocking the air out of her.

She gasped, but it was a hollow sound, devoid of any air. She couldn't breathe. Her eyes watered, and her stomach tightened in agony. Her lungs were being squeezed shut. She fought to catch her breath, and when she finally did, laid on the floor with the roar of the engine in her ear. Her shoulders already ached, and her hands were numb, her eyes useless behind the blindfold. It was difficult not to succumb to panic.

The only sounds she could distinguish were the low hum of the vehicle and the occasional muttered conversation between the men. As the van drove through unfamiliar streets, Emily concentrated on the vibrations beneath her, the sound of tires rolling over asphalt, and the small shifts of the vehicle. She couldn't differentiate turns from curves in the road or what direction they traveled in, much as she tried, but she could feel the cold air seeping in through cracks, chilling her to the bone, and she could smell the faint scent of leather, mixed with the acrid stench of something old and musty.

She tried to focus on the details, to capture any information she could use later, limited though it may now be. The road seemed to twist and turn, stretching on endlessly. They must be out of the city now. Her stomach churned, and the bile rose in her throat as the van made a sudden stop. Her mind spun with questions—where were they? What were they planning to do? Why her?

The doors opened, and she felt the men grab her together and drag her from the van. She couldn't be sure, but it appeared night had fallen. There was little light behind the blindfold, and the temperature was noticeably cooler. They pushed her to her feet, shoving her forward even as she stumbled, trying to catch her balance. Her body ached from the beating, but there was no time to focus on the pain. She had to survive. She had to find a way out.

They shoved her inside a building, and the space was cold, industrial, and unfamiliar. Her mind raced to memorize every detail. The sound of her feet scuffing against the concrete echoed in the empty space. The men threw her into a small room, its icy walls and harsh, bare fluorescent lights only making the atmosphere more suffocating. There were no windows, and the only furniture was a battered chair and a metal table against the wall. There was a faint smell of oil and rust in the air, and the overhead light flickered intermittently, casting sharp shadows across the walls.

The men left her there on the floor, bound and blindfolded, and slammed the door behind them. She was trembling now—a chill creeping over her body as she lay against the cold floor. She could hear voices outside the door, but they were too far away to make out any words. Pressing her face to the ground, Emily used the uneven texture to scrape the blindfold off her eyes and down her face. It was still around her jaw, but at least now she could see.

She wiggled her body across the room, pressing her ear to the door.

"...not going to work."

"...the contract..."

"More is going to come—"

"Fucking idiot!"

"If we kill her..."

"...he'll...do it..."

Emily's mind worked quickly, desperately trying to put any clues together, anything that could get her out of this. They spoke about a contract. One of them thought the other was clearly an idiot, and perhaps a third and fourth voice argued that they should just kill her. But who were they? Why did she matter to them? And what more was going to come?

Then, like a light bulb exploding, she realized.

More wasn't coming.

Moore was coming.

Devlin Moore.

They didn't want her. They wanted him, or whatever they thought he would give them. Something about a contract, she knew that much. They were using her as a pawn, but they didn't know how little Devlin actually cared about her. Whatever they thought, he wasn't coming to save her. Emily needed to think, to escape.

She pulled against her restraints, testing their strength, twisting her wrists against the thick plastic. She wasn't delusional enough to think she could loosen or break them, but maybe if she found the right angle, dislocated the right finger, she could get free. Then she could make a run for it. But all she managed to do was make the plastic cut into her skin, every movement only digging it deeper into her skin. Blood dripped down her hands, smearing onto the floor behind her.

Outside the door, shoes scuffed against the concrete. The door opened, and one of the men stepped inside. He was the slimmer of the two who'd taken her, his build the only differentiating detail between the men's all-black clothes and masks. Emily froze, holding her breath, but it was too late.

"Don't even think about it," the man sneered.

He stepped forward, and her eyes widened as he jabbed a needle into her neck. A cold, sharp pain exploded in her neck, and then a warm heaviness seemed to cover her life a blanket of darkness. Her body went limp, a wave of dizziness flooding over her, and she collapsed on the floor.

"You're not going anywhere," he muttered, his voice a distant echo as everything around her blurred. She fought to remain conscious. She tried to scream, but no sound would leave her lips. Her vision faded to black, and the world around her went silent.

18

———

Devlin sat alone in the parlor, the swirling amber liquid in his glass catching the soft light from the chandelier. He let it roll over the ice, his eyes following its movement. The cold, smooth glass was the only thing grounding him in a world that slipped further away.

The quiet hum of the house was suffocating. It was too still, too quiet. His mind raced, tracing the same painful thoughts over and over again. At one point, he'd had everything under control, every detail accounted for. He had hired Emily for a reason—to sort through the pieces of his life he'd ignored for far too long. It had been years. It was time to move forward, if not to host the extravagant parties of his mother's heyday, at least to stop having to avoid half the rooms in his own home. He had told himself it was about organization, about managing the chaos of his world, but that had been a lie. He'd lied to himself about why he needed her.

Maybe not initially, but his reasons for hiring her and those for keeping her had quickly diverged. It wasn't just her ability to put his life in order; it was her presence. It was the way she'd made him feel something. And that terrified him.

Devlin saw how much he'd let fear dictate his actions, but in the quiet of his thoughts, he realized how much he had been lying to himself. He wanted her. He needed her. But he couldn't have her. Not in his world. Not when danger was always just around the corner.

And so he'd pushed her away. He'd abandoned her, rejected her attempts to connect after such deep and powerful intimacy. Then he'd hurt her, and when she protested his ill treatment of her, he'd lost his temper and struck her. Hard and without mercy. What kind of beast did that to the woman he loved?!

He balked at the thought. *Did he love her?* Was he capable of such a feeling anymore? His stomach turned to rock.

The knock at the front door snapped him out of his thoughts. He set the glass down on the table, the ice clinking in protest, and pushed himself to his feet. Every step felt heavier than the last. His mind wasn't focused on the door or on the visitor. He couldn't care less about who it was. All he could think about what Emily.

He reached for the door handle, his fingers cold against the black metal. Before he could pull it open, his phone buzzed in his pocket. He paused. He pulled it from his pocket and looked at the screen. It was Kara.

He answered it with a sharp swipe, his voice low and tight. "What is it?"

Kara didn't waste time. "We found the bodies of Emily's security detail. Outside her apartment."

The words hit him like a slap, and he froze. His blood ran cold, but he didn't respond to her. He didn't need to. His heart raced, his chest tightened, and his stomach churned. Another knock on the door echoed over the roaring in his ears. He flung the door wide and saw Zoe, Emily's roommate, standing on his stoop, pale-faced with eyes filled with frantic worry.

"Where's Emily?" Zoe demanded, her voice shaking with anger and fear.

The moment she spoke, the knot in Devlin's stomach tightened. Kara kept talking, but he couldn't hear what she said, he didn't need her questions, and he sure as hell didn't need any of her words to know what had happened. It hit him like a punch to the gut, the realization crashing over him. Emily had been taken. They'd gone after her. Just as they'd promised.

He said nothing, his mind already spinning. His fingers dug into the door frame, and he pressed a button on his phone, ending the call. Without a word, he grabbed Zoe's arm and pulled her inside roughly, slamming the door behind her.

"Where is she?" Zoe pressed.

Devlin's mind raced, but the words wouldn't come. He

was paralyzed, locked in a storm of thoughts that only added to the panic clawing at his insides. He looked at Zoe, his jaw clenched so tight it hurt. Zoe was talking, but the words faded in the background as he tried to process everything.

"She—she called me," Zoe said, her words stumbling over each other. "She left a voicemail. She was upset, crying. She said something about a fight with you, but she hasn't answered her phone since then. Her car's still at her apartment, and I found her keys sitting on the sidewalk, but she's gone."

Gone.

The roaring in his ears grew to that of a freight train blaring at a car stopped on its tracks. His world spun out of control, his entire system spiraling out. He'd known something like this could happen. He'd been waiting for this moment. Waiting for the inevitable to happen and bring his world crashing down. If only he'd listened to his gut sooner. If only he'd stayed away from her. This wouldn't be happening.

When Zoe lost her patience and yelled, it finally broke through the fog. "Devlin, what the hell is going on?"

He didn't answer right away, and then his phone buzzed again, the screen flashing with a text from an unknown number.

You have 2 hours to fulfill your contract.

Devlin's heart stopped, the blood draining from his

face. Two hours. Two hours to fulfill a contract with the twins, because while he'd suspected they were responsible, he knew now without a doubt it was them. He'd walked away from no other contract. And if he didn't hold up his end of the deal, they'd kill her.

Or so they thought.

Panic and guilt turned into raw aggression like lava hardening into stone. They gave him two hours to fulfill the contract, which meant he had two hours to find out where they held Emily captive...

And kill them.

No one laid a hand on what was his. He wouldn't let another woman he cared for be killed by his failure. She could go on hating him forever. He wouldn't blame her for it for a moment. But she'd do it alive.

Zoe stepped closer, her eyes searching his face. "Should we call the police?" she asked, her voice trembling slightly.

Devlin shot her an incredulous look. "No police," he muttered, his voice dark, his tone final.

Zoe swallowed, her gaze dropping to the floor. She knew what he meant. She could see the change in him, the shift from panic and disconnection into the controlled man who would stop at nothing to protect what was his.

Devlin's mind was a whirlwind of thoughts, but one thing was clear: he would not let them hurt Emily. He would not let her become another casualty of his past. There was no need for him to explain himself. He wasn't asking for permission, and he didn't care who he had to go through. He was going to get her back.

Zoe watched as Devlin's expression hardened, his eyes darkening with a determination that was genuinely terrifying. She'd heard stories of the cold, distant billionaire who infatuated her friend, and honestly, she hadn't liked him. She liked him even less now. But he was standing in front of her looking like a man who was about to set the world on fire and watch it burn.

Zoe hesitated for a moment, her voice uncertain. "You're in love with her, aren't you?" she asked as the realization hit her.

Devlin didn't answer. He didn't need to. His eyes spoke for him. They were hard, unyielding, and full of something that was darker than anything she had ever seen before.

"She's mine."

The loud groaning of the steel doors as he pushed them open would've been an unfortunate announcement for anyone trying to surprise their enemy, so it was a good thing that Devlin didn't give a shit about that.

The warehouse reeked of oil and sweat and grease, the scent so offensive it had his nostrils flaring in protest. Devlin moved into the building with a sureness that came from knowing you're the most dangerous predator in the jungle with no need to prove it to anyone. Concrete walls stretched high around him, and thick rusted beams arched across the ceiling. The only sounds were the low hum of a flickering overhead light and the muffled shuffle of boots on concrete from somewhere ahead.

He moved as if he belonged there, surprised that they had not stationed a lookout, so sure were they that he would give in to their demands. They thought he wouldn't come. They thought they knew what kind of man he was. That he'd sit back and swallow their threats like a good little heir to a crime-ridden dynasty.

They were wrong.

Devlin rounded a corner and at last spotted one of the twins' men. The man turned, and that was the end of him. Devlin pulled a thick knife from his waistband and lunged before the man could raise his weapon. He gurgled as blood poured from the gash at his neck, his body crumpling where he stood.

A man across the way shouted and pointed at Devlin, who brushed at the spot of blood that had splattered onto his white button-up. He looked up with a raised brow to see the man raise a gun. Without hesitation, Devlin switched the knife to his left hand and drew a 9 mm gun from a holster on his hip.

He brought the gun up and fired. The bullet hit the man in the shoulder, and Devlin swore as the man returned fire, a bullet whirring past his ear. He was out of practice. Firing again, he dropped the man just as two more, a man and a woman, surged from a side hallway, but Devlin was already moving, slipping into the chaos like a blade through flesh. His body was all muscle and purpose, built for the brutality he'd spent his whole life trying to cage.

This was no longer about a contract. This was a message.

He fired a shot at the man, hitting him in the chest and watching him crumple to the floor. He swung his blade toward the woman's belly, but she dodged it and swung a fist hard into Devlin's face, her knuckles connecting with his jaw with a sickening crack. The punch was a stunning blow that split open the inside of Devlin's cheek, but it most certainly broke the woman's hand, so there was some consolation in that.

Devlin raised his gun and fired three shots into the woman's stomach, kicking her away as he continued walking down the hallway. More blood splatter painted his shirt, and he spit a mouthful of his own on the ground, using his shirtsleeve, rolled to the elbow, to wipe the residue from his lips.

Shouts echoed from deeper in the warehouse, but there were only so many places to hide. He knew this hallway went little farther. Wherever they were keeping Emily, it couldn't be much farther. He walked with his gaze fixed on the end of the hallway, his mind fixated on thoughts of her.

He didn't see the man creep up behind him, didn't hear a single step he took, until he looked into one of the side rooms off to his left and caught a sliver of him in his periphery. Before he could do more than twist his body away, the man was close enough to swipe a knife at him. It caught him in the side, slicing through his shirt and into the soft flesh beneath.

Blood poured from the wound, and he groaned as pain exploded in his side. He lunged at the man, but the man caught his gun arm and knocked the knife in Devlin's other hand to the ground. The man reared back to stab him again, but Devlin grabbed him by the throat and pinned him to the wall. The man dropped his weapon, hands clawing at his throat, feet kicking at Devlin's legs as if the pain would bother him at all. He pressed the gun to the man's head and hissed, "Where is she?"

He spat at him.

"That was ill-advised." Devlin wiped his face with his sleeve.

"Do it. I'm not afraid to die," the man said, gasping for breath between each word.

He pushed the gun into its holster, Devlin's other hand never leaving his throat. "But you are afraid of pain."

Fear flashed in the man's eyes, but a voice echoing across the warehouse drew their attention away. Any thought he may have had about telling Devlin what he wanted to know and saving himself was gone the moment he caught sight of a man dressed all in black walking briskly down a long staircase.

It was one of the twins; Liam, Devlin guessed from the look of him.

"Mr. Moore," Liam repeated.

He didn't take his gaze away from the man against the wall. "You have fifteen seconds." Devlin's right hand joined his left at the man's neck, and he slammed the man's head against the wall. He cried out, lashing out at Devlin with feet and fists.

"Fuck you!" the man yelled, his fist connecting with the wound at Devlin's side.

Devlin groaned. "Ten seconds. Where is she?"

"Go to hell," he gasped.

Devlin slammed the man's head into the wall again, and he groaned. Devlin turned to watch Liam walk down the hall, his steps unhurried. Keeping his eyes locked with Liam's, he slammed the man's head into the wall again and again in time with his steps. Liam stopped just a few feet away, crossing his arms and daring Devlin to continue.

When the man's noises ceased and his kicks became twitches, Devlin released him and let the body crumple to the floor, its head caved in and unrecognizable. Devlin wiped the blood from his face with his shirtsleeve. He turned to face Liam.

"You came," Liam said, his tone matter of fact.

"Give me the girl or I'll kill you, your brother, and every other person stupid enough to work for you."

"I don't think so," Liam said, looking pointedly at the blood that seeped from his side. He turned his mouth to the side and called out to someone behind him. "Bring her out!"

From somewhere on the side of the warehouse, a door opened, and a man dragged Emily out. Her arms were bound behind her back, and what had probably been a blindfold was wrapped around her neck. Her dark hair tangled like a dirty halo around a face smeared with grime. His stomach hitched at the purple bruise forming across one cheek, a bruise he'd put there.

Holding her arms and positioning himself behind Emily, a man in black stood, clutching her tightly with one hand, a pistol aimed at her temple with the other. Emily wasn't looking at any of them. Instead, her head drooped, as if she were the ever-complacent human shield, but Devlin knew better. He could tell something was wrong—she shuffled and stumbled as if drunk—but he could see her eyes scanning everything from floor to wall. She was looking for a weapon... or an escape.

That's my girl, he thought.

"I was wondering where you were hiding," Devlin said to the man holding Emily. It was Logan, Liam's twin brother and the other half of this children's circus of a criminal operation.

At the sound of his voice, Emily's head shot up, and her gaze locked with his. Surprise, disbelief, and relief all flashed across her face, but she hid it quickly.

"You should've stayed away, Moore!" Logan spat, dragging Emily backward as a human shield. "You think this changes anything? Your father would've cut a deal. He knew better than to act like a goddamn animal."

Devlin's jaw twitched at the insult, and he looked down at the blood spattered across his shirt. He looked back up at the twins and shrugged. "I'm not my father."

Logan sneered. "You're damn right you're not."

Devlin raised his gun, his eyes locked on Emily's, and pointed it at Logan. In response, Liam drew his gun. He was smarter than his brother, though, and he pointed it right at Emily. He knew Devlin well enough to know he'd take the bullet to save her.

Emily shook her head, and a wave of fresh guilt washed over him. Even after everything he'd done to her, even though she was only here because of him, she didn't want him to sacrifice himself for her. When he didn't respond, he watched her take a deep breath and close her eyes. He couldn't fail her.

Without warning, he turned his gun on Liam and took the shot.

Clean. Perfect. Liam dropped, blood blooming across his chest like a grotesque rose, and the next seconds seemed to stretch into hours. Logan bellowed in pain, shock, disbelief. He turned his gun on Devlin in a rage, forgetting about Emily altogether, just as Devlin had hoped he would.

Both guns exploded with bullets until their clips were empty, the acrid smell of fresh gunpowder masking the smell of grease and blood if only for a moment. A scream echoed off the walls, and when the smoke cleared, Devlin stood with a fresh bullet wound in the shoulder, and Logan lay on the ground at Emily's feet, blood sputtering from his mouth with every breath he took.

Devlin walked over to him, ignoring the blood that seeped from his own shoulder. He knelt down beside Logan, looking at him with disgust. He grabbed the knife from Logan's belt, pressing it against the man's throat.

"Maybe I'm an animal after all," he said, and he drew the blade across Logan's skin, watching as the blood puddled beneath him and his gurgling breaths ceased.

It wasn't quick. It wasn't clean. But it was done.

Devlin's breathing was heavy, ragged, when he turned back toward her. Emily was on the floor, eyes wide, lips parted, her chest rising and falling in rapid bursts. She didn't look away from him. Didn't flinch. She just stared.

He reached for her, his bloodied hands trembling now as he pulled her into his lap, using the knife to cut the zip ties from her wrists. Devlin untied the blindfold and pulled it free of her neck, running his hands over her body and checking her injuries. He was silent, his touch slow, gentle, reverent as if she were made of glass.

Her voice was barely a whisper. "You came."

His jaw clenched. "I should've come sooner."

She looked at his torso. "You're bleeding."

"So are you."

He cupped her face, searching her expression for any trace of fear. There was none, only a questioning look in her eyes. He traced her cheek, his finger brushing lightly over the color there.

"I'm sorry I hurt you." His eyes met hers again, and they both knew he was talking about more than the bruise. "I'll never lay a hand on you again. I promise. No one will. Ever."

Despite their circumstances and her current proximity to more than one dead body, Emily refused to let him off easy. "You know they say abusive partners always say that, and they always do it again."

He sucked in a breath and closed his eyes, letting his hand drop from her cheek. "I deserve that."

"You do. It's your job to protect me from the rest of the world, not from yourself. You're supposed to be my safe place," she said, grabbing his hand and putting it to her cheek. She closed her eyes and leaned into it, inhaling deeply for the first time in hours.

He pulled her to him then, his hand pushing through her hair to cup the base of her neck. "I will be. Every day until the end of days."

His mouth met hers in a kiss that burned—possessive, unrelenting. She clung to him, her hands finding the back of his neck, threading into his hair, pulling him closer. Her breath trembled against his lips, and when their tongues met, they tasted of salt and blood.

She should've been scared.

Instead, she kissed him as if he were her salvation.

He buried his face in the crook of her neck. The scent of her, the warmth of her, was the only thing anchoring him to reality. She ran her fingers down his chest, over his blood-soaked shirt, and he growled low in his throat.

"Emily," he rasped. "I need you."

Her only answer was to kiss him again, deeper this time, hungrier. She lay down with her arms open in invitation, not caring about the pools of blood around them—blood that was cool and sticky on her back—the blood that covered his body. She needed him as desperately as he needed her.

He covered her body with his, groaning at how good it felt to have her under him. His mouth traveled from her lips to her neck, and he lapped at the line of blood there. She sucked in a sharp breath at the stinging pleasure. The taste of her mingled with the metallic taste in his mouth. She panted underneath him, her hips writhing against his.

Hands streaked with blood, none of it hers, dug into his neck, back, hips.

"I can't be gentle," he groaned.

"I don't want gentle."

With a growl, he tore at their clothes until there was just enough out of the way that he could sink into her, and he did. In one powerful thrust, he rammed his cock deep into her, pausing when he was completely embedded to feel her throb around him. And then he was moving, slamming into her to the rhythm of their frantic breaths, pushing her leg up to allow him even deeper.

His teeth clamped on the skin of her shoulder, a beast possessed by the feral need to mark and claim what was his. They moved together, driving each other higher and higher until they exploded together in delicious ecstasy, collapsing into each other in a tangle of limbs and spent passion.

And there, among the carnage that surrounded them, a light glowed, pushing back the shadows of their past and making way for a future dreamed up by the beauty and protected by the beast.

EPILOGUE

For a bonus epilogue and exclusive character art, visit
SelenaCollins.com/spell